STRANGE TALES OF A COTSWOLD TOWN

Also by Denys S. Sissons:

Murder is no Accident

STRANGE TALES
OF A
COTSWOLD TOWN

Denys S. Sissons

UNITED WRITERS
Cornwall

UNITED WRITERS PUBLICATIONS LTD
Ailsa, Castle Gate, Penzance, Cornwall.

British Library Cataloguing in Publication Data:
A catalogue record for this book is
available from the British Library.

ISBN 1 85200 109 7

The characters and incident settings in this book
are entirely imaginary and bear no relation
to any living person or actual place.

Printed in Great Britain by
United Writers Publications Ltd
Cornwall.

To Celia
with grateful thanks for her help.

Contents

I

Old Rectory Close

Old Rectory Close is one of those locations that people always think they recognise when they hear the name, but never quite know where it is. In actual fact it lies to the left of the main road out of town. I won't say which main road, but a quick perusal of the town map should settle that point.

It's a typical suburban close, I suppose – a cul-de-sac, leading to a small group of houses, in several blocks of three, four or five. They call them 'town houses' these days: a euphemism, as everyone knows, for what used to be known as terraced properties. The modern world can be very deceitful.

Each house has three storeys – utility room and garage on the ground floor, living-room and kitchen on the one above, bedrooms and usual offices (excuse the estate agents' jargon) on the top floor. The houses were built around 1960, solidly and well, and on the whole may be regarded as desirable dwelling-places. They are, of course, not suitable for large families, but are ideal for couples without children such as my wife Elizabeth and myself – or perhaps with just one child. The communal gardens are well-maintained by a firm of contract gardeners (this I, for one, regard as a blessing!), the rates and general upkeep are reasonable; there is full gas central heating, double glazing, adequate insulation and friendly neighbours. What more could one want?

I do not propose to reveal which of the fifteen houses in the development is involved in this little tale, because for one thing it is not particularly relevant, and for another neither my wife nor I wish to be hounded and harassed by reporters, sightseers, and others of a sensational inclination. Maybe, when you have read this, you will form your own opinion as to which one it is; if you can do so then I beg you not to reveal the secret. Nor will it be any use to call or telephone: neither Elizabeth nor I will have anything to add to what I am going to tell you now.

It will not take me long to recount my story: there is no long-drawn-out series of connected (or disconnected) events which some enterprising author might turn into a full-scale novel, with sufficient padding. There was only one occurrence, and ever since I have often wondered whether it actually took place, or whether I was the victim of a very real hallucination, or a particularly vivid dream, the product perhaps of an over-excited imagination – or the consequences of an over-indulgence in bread and cheese the night before.

However, enough of this speculation. Read on and you will be able to judge for yourself.

The incident occurred on a Friday, about one o'clock in the morning. There was only my wife and I in the house: our daughter is at college, studying to be a veterinary surgeon, and her room is vacant. We had friends in for the evening, a business colleague and his wife. Bill and I both work for a large manufacturing company situated in a town some seven miles away: I'm on the sales side and he's in personnel. The reason I give this apparently irrelevant information is mainly to show, or attempt to show, that I am in normal circumstances a fairly level-headed chap: one has to be, to keep track of developments in sales management, particularly where the use of computers is concerned. In other words, I don't make a habit of seeing ghosts. Although, as I indicated earlier, I'm not yet certain it was a ghost. And yet – what else could it have been?

Neither my wife nor I indulge in alcohol, only perhaps on social occasions and not in any great quantity. But our friends are

not averse to a noggin or two – especially Bill – and so it has to
be admitted that we imbibed fairly freely during the evening. Bill
and I were on lager, the women on shorts. The result of taking on
this additional liquid was that I had only been asleep for an hour
when I woke up to find that nature called, with a summons that
could not be denied. I glanced at my bedside clock. It was not
long after one o'clock (our friends had departed at midnight and
we had come to bed straight away). I tried to clear the fog of sleep
from my brain, threw back the bedclothes, swung my legs out of
bed and felt for my slippers. I yawned as I rose to my feet, and
my eyes were only half-open as I quitted the bedroom and walked
along the passage towards the bathroom. It was a chilly night and
I was wearing a white winceyette night-shirt recently purchased
for me by my wife as a birthday present, so I had felt duty-bound
to use it now and then. It was, I hasten to admit, a trifle draughty
about the nether regions, but otherwise it was reasonably
wearable.

On the return journey, I was about half-way between bathroom
and bedroom when, for no apparent reason, I seemed to stumble.
At the time I had no real idea of what had happened, but
afterwards I came to the conclusion that it had felt for all the
world as though I had abruptly descended some three or four
inches. I staggered, and instinctively grasped at the banister-rail
overlooking our narrow stairway leading down to the living-room
on the floor below. As my fingers established contact, and I
tightened my grip, I was at first puzzled. It felt . . . different. I
must explain that our handrail is square in section, flat on top and
slightly rough to the touch. The one now under my fingers was
none of these. It was not square in section, it was rounded on top,
and it was smooth and in fact highly-polished. The night was not
completely dark and a faint glimmer of light came through the
open door of the bedroom, emanating from the uncurtained
windows. I looked down, alarm bells ringing. The handrail I
clutched was black, gleaming, thicker than ours, a different shape
altogether. My heart gave a great bound as I realised that, without
any question, it was NOT our handrail at all!

My mind groped with the notion that something was

seriously amiss.

I looked round me, and gradually it dawned on me that I was no longer standing in our passage. Instead, I was in a wide corridor, with black polished boards beneath my feet: our blue Axminster fitted carpet had vanished. There was a faint light coming from below. The corridor went past the top of a wide staircase and several closed doors before it made an abrupt right-hand turn into the black mouth of another corridor. The wallpaper was a heavily-embossed pattern of gold leaves on a maroon background. There were dark pictures in sombre frames at intervals. The doors were of solid black oak.

None of it – not one single aspect – was remotely familiar.

I suppose I was utterly stunned by this sudden and total change to my environment and I stood rooted to the spot, my head spinning. I was no longer asleep, but my brain was not functioning properly. I had no idea where I was, or what was happening. I could hear my heart thumping, much louder than usual, and my blood was like ice in my veins.

It almost froze as my ears caught a faint sound from below, a sound a bit like the shuffling of papers. Somehow I summoned up the necessary will and mobility to move forward until I was in a position to look over the banisters. I stood clutching the unfamiliar handrail and gazed down onto a scene that was utterly alien to me.

Don't misunderstand me. What lay below was nothing abnormal, bizarre or macabre. I looked down into a large spacious hall, with a polished wooden floor covered here and there with dark red rugs, and containing a number of pieces of old-fashioned furniture – the sort one sees in antique shops. There was a massive sideboard, a huge hall-stand with several hats and cloaks on the pegs, an oaken seat, a carved chinese gong, and three or four high-backed chairs. Several doors opened off this room and one of them – almost opposite where I was standing – opened onto another room that, judging by the bookshelves lining the walls, and the heavy mahogany desk in the centre, was a study. I was able to observe all this detail because, hidden from my view, there was a fire in the room, clearly a real coal fire, and the firelight flickered redly on the mature wood of the desk and the serried rows of books.

At the desk sat a man, writing. Even from that distance I could see he was large and heavily-built. He appeared elderly, possibly in his late fifties, and he was clad in clerical attire. His face, what little I could see of it, was heavy and florid, with abundant sideburns turning grey. The hair on his head was scanty and there was a bald patch on his crown, visible because he was bent over the desk-surface. I could hear a faint scratching as he wielded a quill pen which he dipped every now and then into an inkpot set in a massive brass inkstand.

I was completely paralysed and speechless. This complete change in my surroundings, this abrupt transference of myself to what was apparently a bygone time and place, this appearance of a clerical person who was unknown to me, had effectively both immobilised and silenced me. I could only stand and watch him as he wrote, marvelling at the strange but undeniable fact that both he and his surroundings appeared solid and substantial. Yet gradually the idea was burgeoning in my mind that nothing I could see or hear was real, that what lay in front of my bulging eyes was a phantasm, a figment of my disordered imagination, a vision conjured up out of the air that would soon fade.

At that precise moment the man below looked up from his writing. Even then I do not believe that he saw me, but his sudden movement made me draw back from the handrail and as I did so my foot trod on a loose floorboard which emitted a slight creak. He lifted his head higher and, as I waited in breathless suspense, my heart pounding even harder and my mouth dry, his gaze climbed to my face. For a moment that seemed an eternity our gazes locked. I was acutely aware of his fixed regard, of his immobility, of the overall profound silence. Then without warning – his eyes widened, he clutched at the edge of his desk and levered himself to his feet. His face was ashen, his eyes starting from their sockets. He trembled quite visibly and, raising his right arm, he pointed at me with a quivering finger. His mouth opened, his lips moved – and in that instant my surroundings began to spin round me. The study, the hall, the desk, the man, the stairway: all spun dizzily, shimmered in the red-flecked darkness, vanished from my sight. I seemed – God alone knows how – to lift three or four inches, and the next second I was standing on carpet, my hands clutching at our familiar square-topped slightly-rough handrail and looking down the dark narrow stairs to our living-room, a faint glow coming from the television set on standby. Our bedroom lay ahead, the bathroom behind: all was normality once again.

I took a few minutes to take it all in. When I felt able to move and think rationally, I switched on the landing light and descended the stairs to the living-room. It was quiet, dark and empty. I peered into the kitchen, where our cat lay asleep in her basket. I even went down to the ground floor to check that all was well. Then I made my shaky way back to the bedroom, where I found Elizabeth still asleep (it takes a lot to wake her up), sat on the bed and thought long and hard about what had happened. Looking at the bedside clock, I saw that only a few minutes had elapsed since waking up. And yet, in those few minutes, something strange and inexplicable had occurred, something so bizarre that my brain refused to accept it. I was in such a state that, when Elizabeth stirred in her sleep, I nearly jumped out of my skin. She looked so peaceful asleep that I forbore to awake her. I tumbled into bed, but sleep did not easily visit me, and dawn was flushing the eastern sky when I finally dropped off.

The following morning, as I faced Elizabeth over the cereal, I could hardly believe that anything had happened during the night. Had I really seen that man writing in his study – or had it been merely a vivid dream? If indeed it was the latter then it was like no other dream I had ever had: every detail of the man and his surroundings was still firmly etched in my mind. I was so lost in my ponderings that Elizabeth noticed my preoccupation and requested an explanation. Although I had an uneasy feeling that she would not believe me, I was desperately keen on a second opinion and, after a short inner struggle, gave her a brief account of what had transpired. She listened in silence and with surprising calm and, when I had finished, she did not express any doubts, nor did she draw my attention to the fact that I had the previous evening drunk a little more than was usual – *and* made free use of the Camembert. But she did question me about the way I felt and suggested a visit to our doctor, in case I needed a tonic. I did not quite see how a medical man might help, but Ian Peabody GP is by way of being a friend as well as our doctor, so after breakfast I telephoned for an appointment.

I saw him a day or two later and sat in front of his untidy desk and recounted my adventure.

He listened, as my wife had done, in complete silence, then gave me a rapid but – as far as I could judge – thorough examination. Then he sat and regarded me thoughtfully. After a while I said, a trifle irritably, "Well?"

"Yes," he responded. "You are well. Despite the thoroughly licentious life you lead."

Since he is fully aware just how lacking in licentiousness my life is, I ignored his remark but said, a wee bit testily, "I'm delighted to hear it. But what about my story?"

"Ah yes, your story. Well, you've come to the right place, at least."

"Prove it, by saying something sensible."

"Right. I'm prepared to state, in front of witnesses, that I believe every word of it."

"You do!" I exclaimed, gratified.

"Particularly," he went on serenely, "as I don't consider you have the necessary imagination to make up such a tale."

"Oh."

"Anyway, enough of the levity. You've come to me for an explanation and I think I may have one." Ignoring my ejaculation of surprise, he added, "You stated, did you not, that the figure you saw seated at the desk wore what you described as clerical attire? Yes, I thought so. Would you therefore agree that he was most probably a church dignitary?"

"That would seem to be an appropriate conclusion," I said with slight sarcasm.

"Such as, for instance, a rector?"

"Possibly. But why pick on a rector?"

"Because, in the good old days, when things were much more

ordered than they are now, a rector lived in a rectory."

"Again, a reasonable hypothesis. But what . . . *Oh!*"

"Exactly. As you astutely remark, oh. You live in Old Rectory Close. Have you never wondered why it is so called?"

"Well, I've always taken it for granted that a rectory once stood on the site. In fact, I'm sure someone once told me so. But I've never bothered to check on it."

"All of what is now Old Rectory Close was once the grounds of a large rectory. It was pulled down shortly after the end of the last war, but the builder who intended to develop the site died before he could do so, and it was not until the sixties that your houses were built. Apart from a brief spell during the war, when it was used to house refugees from the London blitz, the rectory had been empty ever since 1929 when the Reverend Arthur Devenish, then the incumbent, died of a heart attack."

"That's interesting. But how is it you know all this?"

"As you know, my father was a doctor before me, and this was his practice in the 1920s. The Rev. Devenish was one of his patients."

This, I decided, was not surprising. Ours is not a large town, and the Peabody practice is the local one.

"You say it remained empty after – after this unfortunate happening?"

"Yes."

"Why was that?"

"It gained the reputation of being haunted."

"Ah. Presumably by the – er – ghost of the late rector?"

"On the contrary. It was seeing the ghost that caused him to have the heart attack that finished him off."

"I see," I said slowly. Then I added, "No I don't. I'm a trifle confused. I don't understand what you're saying."

"I'm not very sure I do." He sat in thought for a while, then said, "Let me recount to you in bald detail what happened in 1929. On the fatal night, my father was roused from his bed about 1.30am. I vaguely recall it happening, although I was very young at the time: a loud knocking woke me up as well as everyone else in the house. It was Mrs Dawson, from the rectory, in a very agitated state. After hearing what she had to say, my father dressed, took his little black bag and accompanied her back to the rectory, where he found the Rev. Devenish laid out on the sofa in his study, clearly very near to death. He was being attended by his sister Agatha, a widowed lady who lived in the house. She said she had been in bed, asleep, when she heard her brother give a great cry and then fall. She knew that he had stayed up late, at his desk, to write a sermon for the following Sunday. She went downstairs, to find him lying unconscious on the floor behind the desk in the study. She called the housekeeper and between them they lifted him onto the sofa.

"My father could do little for him. The rector's heart had been none too strong for years and there was no doubt that this attack was a fatal one. My father asked what had triggered it off. The two women could tell him nothing, but the Reverend Devenish revived long enough to whisper an explanation. It appears that he was seated at his desk in his study, engrossed in composition, when he heard a faint creaking noise from the hall. He looked through the open doorway, raised his eyes, and beheld an apparition. He said it was clad in white, and stood motionless up in the gallery overlooking the hall, staring down at him. He said it stood like a corpse, the eyes black and fixed, the face deathly pale. He stumbled to his feet and to his frightened amazement the figure vanished.

"My father never forgot the rector's last words. The dying man raised his head with an effort and whispered, 'When it vanished I knew then it was not a real person, but the Angel of Death come to fetch me away. Therefore I had to go with him.' And with that he died."

When Ian Peabody finished, he and I stared at one another with what I might term 'a wild surmise'.

A few days later I paid a visit to the offices of the County Surveyor and was granted permission to study the plans of the old rectory (still pigeon-holed in the dusty archives) and was able to confirm for myself that what I had suspected was in fact true. The terrace of houses, of which ours was one, had been erected exactly where the rectory had once stood, whilst a few mathematical calculations convinced me that the second-floor passage between our bedroom and our bathroom occupied precisely the same portion of space as that formerly taken up by the gallery on the first floor of the rectory – except that the gallery had been some three or four inches lower.

I mention this not because it furnishes any kind of an explanation – I feel that the incident must of necessity remain inexplicable – but merely as a point of interest.

The only matter that causes me some uneasiness is this: which one of us was the ghost?

II

Greystoke Manor

Few of those people fortunate enough to reside in the Cotswolds can fail to be aware of the existence – or indeed the location – of Greystoke Manor, lying as it does only a few miles north-east of Cheltenham.

It is situated in the midst of some very attractive countryside, well away from main roads and surrounded by well-wooded hills. The fact that it is now used for commercial purposes does not detract from its mellow appearance, or controvert the opinion expressed by many authorities that it is without doubt one of the most impressive and handsome country houses in all England, with a long though relatively unchequered history.

The house was built in the seventeenth century by Osric, 4th Earl of Cardigan. The designer was John Webb, assisted by Anthony Forsyth, whilst some of the ground-floor rooms were decorated by no less a personage than Inigo Jones. Architecturally it follows the Palladian style, then just coming into vogue. The long horizontal lines of the edifice, emphasised by the deep panelled bands between the rows of windows on the ground and first floors, are well balanced by the abnormally large keystones bulking up well above the window-lintels, plus of course the pedimented gables in the east and west wings. The impressive main doorway is a major feature of the house and is by William Wynne.

The 4th Earl of Cardigan was a loyal supporter of the Royalist cause in the Civil War, but alas he found himself on the losing side and lost his head along with Charles 1st in 1649. The following year the victorious Oliver Cromwell gave the house to Sir Edward Parkhurst, one of his staunchest allies. But when James 2nd succeeded Charles 2nd, the struggle between monarch and parliament broke out once more, and when James tried to force Catholicism onto the state, an invitation was sent to William of Orange to come over and take charge. Following the crowning of William III in 1689, Parkhurst was created the 1st Earl of Worcester and, a few years later, he had the house partly rebuilt by the renowned William Talman.

From then on England, and Greystoke Manor, enjoyed more than a hundred years of relative peace and stability, but in 1805 the house passed into the hands of Sir Ranulph Tredington, a wealthy landowner who profited from the beginnings of the Industrial Revolution and made so much money that he was able to finance the Government of the day, in return for which he was made Lord Greystoke. It was his grandson, also named Ranulph, who was owner and occupier of the mansion when the chain of bizarre events that form the next story occurred.

Now, alas, the glory is departed. Early in the twentieth century the house passed into the hands of the Civil Service. In 1969 it was purchased by IPC (the International Pharmaceutical Corporation) and has since then been in almost constant use as a convention centre and teaching college. At least this ensures that the beauty of the exterior, and of the extensive parklands that surround the house, is maintained, whilst of course the Inigo Jones' rooms on the ground floor are sacrosanct and kept inviolate for posterity.

But now to my story.

The Great Oak of Greystoke was, in 1855, known over a wide area, not only for the euphony of its title but also because of its extreme age, size and beauty. It stood, proudly defiant of the passing centuries, just inside the boundary of the vast Greystoke estate and about a mile from the house. It was surrounded by lesser trees as a monarch is attended by his courtiers, and the immediate vicinity abounded with undergrowth, bushes and ferns. Its long thick branches, dense with the greenest-possible foliage in summer, stretched up and out, far above all other trees, a landmark to the country people who lived in the area and a source of pride and joy to the owner, Lord Greystoke, to his wife Charlotte, and in particular to their only son Mark.

At some time in the distant past, an artistically-inclined ancestor of the present owner had been so smitten by the charms of the magnificent tree that he had commissioned a painting of it in oils. Unfortunately his ability to select an artist whose work might grow in stature with the years did not match his wealth: the pale young man who executed the commission never became well-known and eventually he married the daughter of a rich banker and never painted another subject. The resultant picture, passably well-rendered in the manner of a Gainsborough landscape, had hung for many years in the Great Hall at the Manor. Alas: the artist's technical expertise had been on a par with his talent and the canvas had gradually grown darker, grimmer and more cracked with the passing of time, until the subject-matter could only be described as indistinct, and the picture resembled the gloomier efforts of Jacob van Ruisdael and his contemporaries.

In 1843 Greystoke married Charlotte, the elder daughter of the Earl of Cambridge and brought her back to live in the ancestral home. It was she who, aspiring to become a renowned and indeed celebrated hostess and patron of the arts, consigned the picture to one of the attic rooms and replaced it with a superb Madonna and Child by Caravaggio (now in the Uffizi Museum, Florence).

A year later a son was born to them and christened Mark Reginald Ranulph St. Fulk Greystoke. Despite this handicap he grew up into a slender and handsome lad, with long black hair and dark soulful eyes which matched his reserved and almost brooding disposition. Quite soon he displayed considerable intelligence, clearly not inherited from his father, and a sharp sensitivity equally clearly not drawn from his mother. He was far from robust and exhibited not the slightest interest in, nor the faintest liking for, the kind of sports and pastimes his father favoured. Lord Greystoke was a Tory politician when he felt so inclined, but spent the greater part of his time – and a considerable portion of his wealth – engaged in the current preoccupations of the majority of gentlemen landowners in the county: that is to say, hunting, fishing and shooting. He was also addicted to prize-fights and horse-races and lost thousands of guineas in reckless wagers and in general demonstrating that his facility for picking winners was on a par with his lack of facility to do anything worthwhile locally or in Government. He was also extremely partial to the wenches, in particular to the doxies who infested the purlieus of his flat in Chelsea; his frequent and prolonged stays at which he explained away to his wife as necessary to further his ambitions to help rule the country. This fairly patent lie she did not for one moment believe, but she was forced to accept it as an inevitable concomitant to the life into which she had been born.

Thus deprived of a father's time, attention and – it must be admitted – affection, Mark turned to his mother for consolation and it was she who imbued in him an affinity for the gentler aspects of life, and instructed him in art, literature and music. He learned to appreciate paintings by artists who were, even then, acknowledged masters: to read and understand books by the Brontes, plays by Shakespeare, poetry by Keats: to listen to, and later play, piano pieces by Chopin and Mozart. When he was old enough for schooling, his mother and father had a violent and recriminatory argument over what should be done with him, Lord Greystoke favouring Eton and Oxford, his mother determined that her son should not be subjected to the indignities and iniquities that she understood were prevalent at these seats of learning. Surprisingly enough, she won the day and whilst Lord Greystoke retired in high dudgeon to London to seek solace in the arms of his current buxom paramour, she engaged a tutor, a quiet studious young man named Timothy Nightingale.

When Mark was not at his lessons, or playing the grand piano in the music room, he spent much of his time roaming the great house and the extensive estate, preferring his own company to that of other children. No one, not even his doting mother, knew anything of what went on inside that dark-haired head, or behind those large brown eyes. He confided in his mother no more than in his tutor, and never in his father, who at no time was able to bridge the enormous gulf between him and his only son. This same gulf was widened not only by lack of time and empathy but also because it was very clear that Mark was rapidly developing a great affection for and interest in all inhabitants of the animal kingdom and in consequence showed nothing but contempt and hostility towards his father's inclination for blood-sports.

Mark was eleven when he discovered the painting of the Great Oak. At the time he was engaged in one of his favourite occupations, rummaging around in the enormous chaos of bric-a-brac and oddments that filled several of the seldom-visited attics, examining his finds and weaving fantasies about them and their origin. A moth fluttered out from some old garments and made for the top of a wardrobe and in pursuing it (let it be said, not to kill it) he discovered a pile of old pictures half-hidden by dust and cobwebs. He disinterred them, brought them down, dusted them off and idly went through them. As a result of this little encounter, the painting of the Great Oak was selected from the rest and transferred to his bedroom, where Mathers, the second footman, hung it for him, positioning it as directed on the wall at the foot of Mark's bed so that his young master could lie in bed and study it at leisure. This much he revealed to his mother when she remarked on the sudden reappearance of the picture she had last seen some twelve years before, but he did not respond to her enquiry as to why that particular painting had been chosen. It was clear he found the subject intriguing (she was amazed at the amount of time he spent gazing at it) but he could not – or would not – say why. However, a possible answer was indicated one night several weeks later when Mark was tucked up in bed and his mother had just finished reading to him. He confided to her in a sleepy voice that he was fascinated not so much by what he could see as by what he could *not* see – that is, the area concealed by the thick trunk and the dense undergrowth around the base of the tree. When she told him that the answer to that question could easily be ascertained by going to the actual place where the tree was situated, he woke up and exhibited such excitement that she believed he might well have made the journey there and then, and in his nightshirt too. She was forced to restrain him and finally to forbid him to do anything other than go to sleep.

The very next morning he declared his intention of visiting the Great Oak at once, before breakfast and before the arrival of his tutor. His mother gave him strict instructions to return within the hour, but when this time had elapsed, and Timothy Nightingale had arrived to find his pupil absent, Lady Greystoke despatched the young man in pursuit. When later the two returned together, the errant boy pale with anger and frustration at being so summarily disrupted from his desires, he received a severe admonition from his perplexed mother. When the lessons were over, and Mark had again left the house, Lady Greystoke interrogated the tutor.

"I went immediately to the Great Oak as you directed, my lady, and found your son recumbent on the turf beneath the tree," he told her. "In accordance with your wishes, I advised Master Mark that he was to return to the house with me so that I could continue to tutor him."

He was clearly about to say more, but instead closed his lips. She, however, correctly interpreted his hesitation.

"He was reluctant?"

"Extremely so, my lady. I was obliged to coerce him into accompanying me and even then it was apparent that he would return there as soon as he was allowed to do so."

"Which I suspect he has now done."

"I believe so, my lady."

She frowned.

"I have revealed to you how he dotes on that picture of the Great Oak, the one in his room. Recently he expressed to me his desire to know what lay beyond. Would I be correct in assuming that you found him in that place?"

"You would, my lady."

"What particular merit did the area possess?"

"None that I could see, my lady. It was pleasant enough: a

stretch of smooth green sward, sheltered by bushes and fern, shaded by the overhanging branches of the oak, frequented by many birds and small animals. But no more than that."

She frowned again, but in a brief while her brow cleared.

"Very well: perhaps it is no more than a passing fancy. We shall find, no doubt, that in due time he will discover other and more rewarding pursuits. In any event, he is doing little harm whilst there."

"This is so, my lady."

Thus was Master Mark allowed to continue with his preoccupation in connection with the little haven he had evidently chosen as his own. But, as the weeks went by, it soon became apparent to many members of the household as well as to his mother that he was not to be diverted from his fancy by other pastimes. In fact, his interest in the sylvan nook behind the great tree grew so intense that it became in the nature of an obsession. He spent almost every minute of his time there, taking a blanket to lie upon and a book to read, and chafed at the bit when forced to undergo tuition, or even retire to his bedroom for the night. Even here he indulged himself by lying in bed and gazing at the painting, presumably imagining himself at that sequestered spot which by now had to be indelibly etched in his memory.

Eventually Lady Greystoke confessed to her husband that she was less than happy with the situation; she felt that Mark's infatuation for his secret place was by now too intense and he should seek other interests. His father however was as usual involved with his own affairs (especially one with a fresh trollop who lodged conveniently near his apartment in town) and merely commented irritably that, if the boy was happy doing what he was doing, where was the harm and why interfere with what seemed to be a satisfactory arrangement? But his mother remained unconvinced. She was too loving a parent to forbid Mark to do anything without good reason and in any case she had the uneasy feeling that he might go so far as to disobey her, in which case compulsion would be required, and she dreaded to think what that might do to him and to the harmony of family life. She did her best to divert him, giving him a puppy to look after, and finding children of neighbouring landowners for him to play with, and taking him on visits to Bath and Canterbury. But none of her ruses succeeded. Gradually the worry began to affect her health, and one day she felt so unwell that her husband was obliged to summon Dr Walpole, who resided in the village and attended most of the gentry roundabout. The good doctor was a man whose knowledge of the healing arts was more advanced than many of his contemporaries and, instead of attempting to treat the symptoms, took pains to ascertain their primary cause. It was not long before Lady Greystoke was confiding her problem to him. He was thoughtful for a while, then asked to see the boy alone. After having been closeted with Mark for an hour, he returned to his patient's chamber in pensive mood and, in reply to her anxious questions, replied, "By your leave, Ma' am, I am of the considered opinion that there is but one solution open to you. Fortunately it is not difficult and lies, I think, within your compass."

"Tell me this very moment, sirrah."

"Is it not so, Ma'am, that if Adam had taken back from Eve the apple he had offered her, and cast it beyond her reach, the unhappy pair would not have succumbed to the sins of the flesh?"

"Speak not to me in riddles, man: give me plain and simple advice."

"I apologise for my clumsy parable, Ma'am. What I was attempting to advise you was, in brief, to remove the temptation."

"Remove it? How so?"

"Cut down the Great Oak."

"Cut down the Great Oak!" It was as though he had suggested that she become his mistress. "My husband would never permit it."

"In that event, Ma' am, your problem will remain unsolved and could well grow more serious with the passing of time."

Despite the drastic nature of the remedy Dr Walpole had recommended, a seed took root in her mind and, as the days went by and Mark became more and more attached to his private retreat, it grew and flourished. Eventually she felt bold enough to broach the matter to her husband. As expected, he erupted with a typical outbreak of choler and rejected the idea forthwith. Moreover, he was so deeply incensed that he forbad her ever to mention the subject again.

Thus thwarted, she was at her wit's end to know what to do. Then her maid, a young and comely wench named Lucy, suggested with great diffidence that her mistress might care to visit one Abigail O'Mara, an aged woman who resided in a cottage in the forest and was reputed to possess magical powers.

"Folks hereabouts du say she be as old as the hills," said Lucy in a suitably awed voice.

"Such foolishness," responded Lady Greystoke uncertainly.

"And 'tis said that she du know what others may not, du perform what others durst not, du see what others cannot," went on Lucy, ignoring her mistress's comment. "Mayhap she could be of service to your Ladyship."

Lady Greystoke was by now so desperate that she was ready to grasp at the slightest chance.

"Know you where this old crone resides?"

"Aye, m'lady."

"We will journey there tonight. See to it."

Thus the lady of the manor came face to face with the local wise woman in the latter's tiny two-room cottage deep in Greystoke Woods. The whole area, in those days was sparsely populated, and Lady Greystoke had a loaded pistol concealed in her muff in case of an encounter with footpads. Abigail O'Mara turned out to be as ancient and as wizened as Lucy's description of her implied. What hair she had left was white and tousled, a profusion of warts and nodules decorated her crazed visage, and to the visitor's horror she smoked a noisome churchwarden pipe stuffed with some unknown but rank-smelling weed. But she seemed lively enough: her black eyes darted about in their sunken sockets like bees in a parson's pocket and her voice was high-pitched and loud enough to jar Lady Greystoke's sensitive ear-drums. However, the owner of those ear-drums resolutely stifled her dislike of the old woman and her slum-like shack and in a few well-chosen phrases unburdened her soul to the crone.

To her credit, Abigail listened in attentive silence, puffing freely at her nauseous pipe and occasionally scratching herself in unmentionable places. At the end of the recital she nodded and then sat completely immobile – that is, save for a brief suck at her pipe now and again – reminding Lady Greystoke of a small and hideous barbarian idol. Finally Abigail stirred and said, "It can be done, dearie."

"How?" asked Lady Greystoke, stifling her resentment at the term.

"Never you mind your pretty 'ead, dearie. It can be done."

"When?"

"Within seven days."

"I insist upon knowing how you will perform this task."

But the old witch neither spoke nor moved in response to this arrogant announcement. And Lady Greystoke quickly realised that there was little to be gained by insisting on an answer and so rose to her feet. To her revulsion the old crone suddenly fastened bony fingers about her slender wrist.

"You 'aven't 'eard me price yet, dearie."

"Unhand me, you stupid virago, then you may speak. But do not presume to imagine that I am a fool to be held to ransom. Tell me your price and I will tell you if I am prepared to pay it."

The witch released her and said, "It'll be twenty jimmies for that, m'lady: no less and no more."

"Jimmies?"

"Jimmy-o'-goblins, m'lady," Lucy hastened to explain. "Sovereigns."

Lady Greystoke's eyes narrowed.

"A great deal of money for a woman of your sort, I vow."

In return Abigail gave her a sly look and abruptly cackled out loud.

"Wouldn't ye say it were worth it, m' lady?"

Lady Greystoke compressed her lips.

"Very well. You will be given your price – when I am satisfied the deed has been done."

With that she quitted the foetid hovel.

Five nights later a terrible storm broke out in the area. There was thunder, lightning and heavy rain. At around 3am the black night was transformed into glaring day by a tremendous eye-blinding flash of lightning, followed immediately by a horrendous crash of thunder, both more severe than anything that had previously been experienced.

The next day Manners, the estate bailiff, reported with a sorrowful mien that the celebrated Great Oak was no more, having been struck and felled by lightning during the night.

The day after that, Lady Greystoke despatched Lucy to the small cottage in the forest with the fee that she felt Abigail had indisputably earned.

Unfortunately, this did not solve the problem. Thus cruelly and summarily deprived of his beloved haven, Mark turned sullen and unco-operative and became extremely difficult to control. Lady Greystoke's heart sank as she realised that this latest development was due to her own precipitate actions (or so she firmly believed) and also that the drastic remedy applied to the disease was irreversible. She tried her utmost to cope with Mark's new moods, which varied from a sullen depression to a frightening hostility, but in the end her love and patience proved unavailing and she was forced to go to her husband and confess her failure. It was typical of him that he reacted by taking a whip to his son, thrashing him as though punishing one of his dogs. But, so far from improving the situation, it made it far worse: Mark fell into an attitude of stony indifference and took to his bed, recumbent for hours on end and staring almost sightlessly at the painting on the wall. His mother tried to keep this latest development from her husband but even he, still preoccupied as he was with his own affairs (both political and amorous) could not fail to note the boy's absence from the downstairs rooms and his method of resolving this problem was merely a repetition of his earlier effort: he gave the boy a second and more severe thrashing, tore the painting from the wall, and with his own hands took it up to the attics, threw it into a corner of one of the rooms, locked the door and shouted to Mark that he would disown him forthwith if he so much as set his eyes on the picture again.

The next morning Mark was gone.

It was a cold and frosty morning in late January and the boy's absence was first discovered by the junior upstairs maid when she took into his room a jug of hot water. His bed was empty but rumpled, as though it had been slept in; of the boy there was no sign. Assuming that he had risen early and was elsewhere, she did not think to mention it, and the matter only came to light when Mark did not appear for breakfast. Lady Greystoke sent the housekeeper up to investigate. When the latter returned to say that the boy was still absent, Lady Greystoke herself went up to his room, taking the housekeeper with her, to ascertain the facts. She found her son's clothing of the previous day still on the chair where it had been placed the night before. Moreover, the housekeeper was ready to swear that none of his other day-clothes was missing. It was inconceivable that Mark could have ventured out into the bitter cold in his night-shirt and in consequence Lady Greystoke ordered a thorough search of the entire house.

An hour later the housekeeper was obliged to inform her mistress that, despite an intensive search of all the rooms, involving every member of the large staff, there was no trace of the missing boy.

Now deeply perturbed, Lady Greystoke summoned Manners, the estate bailiff, and directed him to use all his men and make a comprehensive search of the grounds, outbuildings, stables, barns, granaries, storerooms, huts, hovels and all other places where an unthinking boy might hide himself.

By midday Manners was able to advise his mistress that the entire estate had been gone through with a fine toothcomb and Mark was not present.

Lady Greystoke was now beside herself with worry, but she maintained sufficient presence of mind to despatch a messenger on the fastest horse in the Greystoke stables to her husband's pied-à-terre in London. By great good fortune (looking at it purely from the noble lord's viewpoint) the current doxy had just been sent away by the time the messenger arrived and Lord Greystoke was discovered indulging in his usual heavy post-coital meal in the company of similarly-minded colleagues. The scared messenger feared a choleric outburst when he made known the reason for his presence, and he was not disappointed. His master's reaction was immediate and violent, an explosion of wrath that took him to the verge of apoplexy and caused the unhappy bearer of the bad news to cringe with abject terror. But when the tide of anger had subsided, Lord Greystoke had no option but to cut short his stay in town and return home to take charge of the matter personally.

He reached Greystoke Manor the following evening to find his wife prostrate in bed with worry, Dr Walpole in attendance, and still no sign of the missing son and heir. The weather was now bitterly cold, the temperature below freezing, the smell of snow in the icy air, and fears were expressed that, if Mark was indeed out and abroad in his night-shirt, he would never survive the night. Accordingly Lord Greystoke, mindful of his position and reputation, set about organising search-parties, in so doing causing many of his neighbours a great deal of surprise by his energy and enterprise. In those far-off days, the police were few in numbers, especially outside the big cities, and their activities were confined to the more lawless of criminals, such as footpads, murderers, sheep-stealers and the like. Missing persons were not their responsibility – nor were they the responsibility of any one individual or body. If a man, woman or child went missing, it was up to the family to pursue the matter as best it could, such efforts being dependent to a large extent on their standing and wealth.

Lord Greystoke had both the standing and the wealth, whilst the eagerness to trace his son stemmed possibly as much from a great urge to beat the living daylights out of him as from parental affection. But he was able to ensure that virtually the entire labouring population of the Manor and surrounding area was engaged in a search throughout the night. Dozens of groups combed the environs of Greystoke Manor and beyond, the flickering lights from their hand-lanterns like a myriad will-o'-the-wisps flitting about the cold clear night, the baying of the bloodhounds brought into play by the noble Lord like that of the hounds of hell.

Next morning, when it was learned that the efforts of the previous night had been in vain, the search was continued, extended and intensified. The estate was again covered by gangs of more-or-less willing helpers, whilst outside the perimeter the men of the village, and of surrounding villages, quartered the countryside, peering, probing, questing, scrutinising, looking this way and that, asking questions. Kidnap by gypsies was feared, but none had been reported in the vicinity. Any unfortunate vagrant found in the district was picked up, roughed up, subjected to beatings and detailed questioning, and then run out of the county.

As the days went by, and no trace of Mark was found, Lord Greystoke had handbills printed and stuck up on every tree, wall, building and post for twenty miles around. He bribed the local constabulary to take part in the hunt. He employed a firm of solicitors in London well-known for their success in locating missing persons and paid them heavily for their well-meaning but futile efforts. But as the passing days accumulated into weeks, and the weeks into months, even his zeal flagged and his resources dwindled. Lady Greystoke was by now convinced that her son was dead and, prostrate with grief, was attended daily by Dr Walpole, who feared for her health and her sanity.

One morning, some time after her son had gone missing, she suddenly quitted her bed of illness and announced without warning that she was going to seek the assistance of the one person who had hitherto not been involved in the proceedings – Abigail O'Mara, the ancient crone who lived in the forest. When Lord Greystoke heard of her intention, he became entirely unreasonable and forbade her to go. But she was totally desperate and stubbornly refused to obey him. He flew into another of his characteristic rages and there was a violent and recriminatory argument in the morning-room, during which the staff listened apprehensively at the door and waited in fear and trembling for the outcome.

They were not disappointed. As Lady Greystoke continued to maintain her stand in the face of her husband's irrational fury and vituperative abuse, he suddenly turned a deep purple in complexion, gave forth a terrible groan, and collapsed. Dr Walpole was summoned and he had the owner of the Manor conveyed to his bed and he applied all the customary and fashionable treatments of the time, meanwhile advising her ladyship that her husband had suffered a stroke and would be restricted to his bedroom for weeks, if not months.

Thus abruptly freed from Lord Greystoke's interdiction and interference, Lady Greystoke decided to carry out her plan. That evening she and Lucy were conveyed by brougham and four to a convenient place and then travelled on foot along the muddy overgrown path that led through the black and silent forest to the small hovel that crouched in its dark tree-encircled clearing like a misshapen animal hiding from the hunt. Abigail was there, huddled in her chair, the same smoke-tarnished pipe jutting from her quivering lips. It was frosty cold and the interior of the hut was inadequately heated by a small peat fire and equally inadequately lit by one single rushlight, the illumination from which had difficulty in piercing the smoke-laden air. Holding a perfumed kerchief to her nose, Lady Greystoke took the only other seat (a decrepit oak milking-stool) and told the hag the reason for her second visit, and asked for assistance. Lucy stayed back in the shadows, keeping watch and ward over her mistress.

"An' what sort o' help was it you'd be a-wantin', m'lady?" Abigail asked in her high-pitched cracked voice.

"I want you to tell me where he is."

" 'Ow long is it since 'e went?"

" 'Tis nigh on six weeks now, I fear."

The old woman's rheumy deepset eyes searched her visitor's face.

"And 'ave you thought, m'lady, 'e might not be a pretty sight when found?"

Lady Greystoke looked aghast. "What mean you, you old witch?"

" 'E could be naught but a corpse, lyin' in a ditch mebbe, 'is young flesh a-moulderin' and worms oozin' from 'is starin' eyes and 'is . . ."

"Stop it!" Lady Greystoke's voice was almost demented. She rose and would have struck the old crone, but something – she could not say what – held her back. Her arm felt curiously paralysed and numb, and after a long moment she sat back on the stool.

The witch cackled. "You don't fancy the idea, eh m'lady? But that's how it might be."

Lady Greystoke shook her head wearily.

"Whatever the answer, I wish to know it. Lies it within your powers?"

"Mebbe, mebbe not. I tries my arts, but promises naught." The bony skull, with its attendant white floss of straggly hair, twisted sideways as the eyes peered at the visitor. "Last visit cost ye a packet, m'lady. This'n'll cost you a whole piece more, you can lay to that."

The other's nose wrinkled with haughty dictate.

"Name your price, witch."

"Twenty jimmies fer tryin' – and fifty more if I find 'im."

"Jimmies? Oh, I understand – sovereigns." The speaker's eyes opened wide and flashed with anger. "You're a damned impudent old harridan! How dare you hold me to ransom thus?" Her gaze narrowed. "I could have you whipped through the streets of Gloucester without any of your filthy rags to protect you. I warrant there would be no need then for payment to loosen your tongue."

But Abigail remained unperturbed, merely shaking her ragged locks.

"You won't do nothin' like that, m'dearie. 'Cause why? 'Cause then you wouldn't get ter know what you want ter know. And 'cause, if you *was* to be so foolish, you might find a whole lot more trouble than you bargained for. I s'pect you calls to mind what 'appened after your last visit, m'lady?"

Lady Greystoke's eyes blazed afresh, but even as she was about to utter an angry and arrogant retort, the thought entered her mind that, if this mangy old fleabag had engineered the destruction of the Great Oak, it would not be beyond her powers to create a great deal of 'unpleasantness' to anybody, however high-born, with whom she crossed swords. In view of her present situation, she felt she could not bear additional burdens and so she contented herself with saying, in a hostile voice, "Twenty sovereigns for your labours, and another twenty if you succeed."

But the aged woman was surprisingly adamant and refused to listen to any lesser offer. Lady Greystoke was unaccustomed to haggling and eventually she submitted with an ill grace and agreed to the terms originally stipulated.

Thereafter events moved rapidly. Lady Greystoke and her maid were banished to one corner whilst the wizened crone, amazingly agile for one of her (alleged) age, cleared a space on the dirt floor in the centre of the hovel, placed on it a mat woven of rushes, squatted before it and cast upon it three small polished white bones and studied the arrangement they made as they fell, meanwhile rocking to and fro and uttering an alien chant in an ululating voice. At the end of this performance she looked at them with a toothless grin.

"The signs be good," she cackled. Putting the bones aside, she placed on the mat a bowl of burnished copper and poured into it small amounts of various powders, some red, some white, some grey, from little flaxen bags. She stirred the resultant concoction with her finger, then leaned across to the fire, plucked from it a glowing splinter and applied it to the contents of the bowl. There was a discreet flash, a flickering of almost invisible flame, and the contents of the bowl burned with a deal of smoke and a pungent but not wholly disagreeable smell. Despite her distress, Lady Greystoke could not help but be intrigued by these esoteric preparations and she noticed that the smoke was not completely normal but seemed to hover above the bowl in a peculiar fashion, and to shift and undulate in a most perplexing way. The hag continued to rock and croon in weird dissonant tones, meanwhile staring at the constantly wavering pall of smoke with bulging eyes.

After some ten minutes, Abigail appeared to pass into a trance, during which her eyes became fixed, wide open and sightless. As this continued, Lady Greystoke grew fidgety and impatient, but somehow she controlled her feelings and forced herself to remain silent. Eventually Abigail's irises enlarged until they all but took over her blood-flecked eyeballs, the latter swelling out like monstrous elderberries. The thin mouth quavered, opened and shut, clearly fighting to get some words out: but all that emerged was a long gusty sigh. As though by this means she had ejected some unclean foetor from her body, she relaxed: her irises returned to normal, her limbs ceased to shake, and finally life and recognition came back into her eyes and she gazed at her visitor.

The latter, puzzled by the look on the witch's face, said in a hoarse whisper, "Saw you my son?"

The head, topped with scanty scraggly white hair, nodded. "I seen 'im," she said with unusual gravity.

Lady Greystoke's heart gave a great leap.

"Where? Where saw you him? Near here? Does he – does he still live and – and breathe? Tell me at once, you witless hag, or I'll have the answers whipped out of your scrawny body."

"Tell me one thing first, m'lady. Was the Great Oak not destroyed – destroyed utterly, once and for all?"

"Yes, yes, it surely was. I saw the result with my own eyes. And you were well-rewarded." Lady Greystoke's eyes drew together. "What scurvy diversion is this, you mangy witch? Durst you trifle with me at this time?" She leapt to her feet, went across to the squatting woman, grasped her bony shoulders and shook her violently. "My son! Where is my son? I can see you have seen him. Where? Where?"

Abigail stared up at her, fear now in her bloodshot eyes.

"I seen 'im," she repeated. "I seen 'im, true as I be squattin' here, a-lyin' under the Great Oak, on 'is back, on a shawl, a-starin' up at the branches."

Lady Greystoke stared down at her and her face was pale. "What sayest you? What madness is this?"

"Madness, is it? Aye, m'lady, you speak the truth of it. For I wot well that the Great Oak was destroyed and is no more. Yet – and I swears this by all the gods of this or any other world – I seen 'im, lyin' under that selfsame tree, like what you tol' me he allas liked to do."

Lady Greystoke tottered backwards, was caught by Lucy and guided back onto the milking-stool, where she subsided, totally bemused.

"I – I understand not what you are saying to me."

"Nor I, m'lady. But I seen 'im, where I says I seen him, and that's all there is to it."

"You swear it was my son?"

"Aye."

"And he – he lived?"

"Ah, now that I couldn't tell. He lay as a log, unmovin'."

"How was he clothed?"

"In a nightshirt, m'lady."

"And saw you – saw you aught else?"

The crone's eyes creased in thought, then opened wide.

" 'E 'ad a book, m'lady. There was a book by 'is side."

"Aught else?"

"No, m'lady. All else was 'id from me." She paused then added, "It were as though I looked into a picture."

Lady Greystoke's brain was numbed by a mixture of shock, bewilderment and disappointment, and she was unable to take in what she had heard. Suddenly she wanted nothing more than to leave that squalid hovel in the cold damp forest and return home, despite the fact that her son was missing and her husband lying on a bed of sickness. She took her purse from Lucy, extracted twenty sovereigns and threw them at Abigail.

" 'Ere!" Expostulated the old hag, staggering to her feet. "This ain't the bargain we struck. There's a sight more'n this to come, I reckon."

"No more!" snapped Lady Greystoke. "And you may consider yourself fortunate that I do not have you behind bars for your fraudulent practices. You have *not* found my son. What you have said to me means naught but trash and I'll not have any more truck with you or your bewitchments."

So saying, she stormed out and, with Lucy hastening after her, made her way back along the path through the forest, pursued by a volley of furious and high-pitched ranting and raving that did not cease to assault her ears until she was in the brougham and being driven back to the Manor.

They were driving between the gates giving entrance to the estate when something that Abigail had said towards the end of the 'consultation' suddenly sprang into her mind – something of which the significance had escaped her at the time but which now struck her like a physical blow.

What was it the witch had said? "All else was 'id from me. It were as though I looked into a picture."

The words burned into her consciousness. Without understanding her motives, she shouted to the coachman to spur his team. Alive to the note of urgency in his mistress's voice, he obeyed with such alacrity that his horses reared up on their hind-legs and the gravel spurted from under the wheels as the brougham thundered towards the main entrance of the Manor. The leather binding of the brakes squealed and smoked as they were violently applied.

Ignoring Lucy's bewilderment, Lady Greystoke dismounted, hastened into the great hall and up the wide curving staircase to the first floor. Arriving at her husband's room, she threw open the door – to find his bed empty and his personal valet tidying up the drawers in a tallboy against the wall.

"Where is your master?"

"Not here, my lady."

"I can see that, you doltish loon." She stared around the room, then back at the frightened servant. "Know you where he keeps the key of the attic wherein he stored the oil painting of the Great Oak?"

"Aye, my lady. It was always kept in the top drawer of this very tallboy."

"Was? You mean it is no longer there?"

"No, my lady. My master took it with him . . . "

"When?"

"Not ten minutes since. He was deeply angry, and disturbed all the contents of the drawer before . . . "

Ignoring him, she ran from the room, only to bump into the housekeeper. Immediately she seized the flustered woman by the arms.

"Know you where my husband is?"

"My lady, how can I be of assistance? You are distraught . . ."

"Answer me, hag, or I'll dismiss you this very instant. Where is my husband?"

"Oh my lady, I do not know what is amiss. He came with fury into my kitchen and demanded to know where was the furnace-room. He was – he was red with passion. Oh my lady, what wants he with the furnace-room?"

Lady Greystoke whirled about and rushed away. She knew the way to the furnace-room, having had on one occasion in the past to steal down there and destroy certain letters that she had not wished her husband to find. She negotiated the steep stone steps down to the cellars without care but also without mishap, and arrived at the dark foetid furnace-room to find Lord Greystoke, clad in nightshirt and overgown, standing before the gaping maw of the furnace, shielding his face from the heat and holding in his free hand a picture which clearly he intended to consign to the metal Moloch's fiery interior.

"No, no!" shrieked Lady Greystoke, rushing up to him and grasping in vain for the picture. "Please – my love – I beg of you – I beseech you – please do not do this – "

"Unhand me, wife!" he shouted. " 'Tis this damned painting is responsible for the foul curse that has befallen the House of Greystoke. Ere our son clapped eyes on this – this accursed daub, all was well. A plague upon it! It must burn – burn – burn in the fires of hell, and then – mayhap – the curse will not endure."

His big frame shuddered as though with the ague and his eyes burned with a fierce, almost insane, light. His wife shrieked hoarsely and fought with him, but he thrust her away and, with one heave of his arm, cast the picture into the white-hot heart of the flames. The old canvas caught fire in the instant and Lady Greystoke, evading her husband's clutch, threw herself down to the open jaws of the furnace. Her starting, bulging eyes searched the rapidly-scorching picture, saw the dark mass of the Great Oak, the wide-spread branches, the green sward beneath the tree, and something else – something that might have been a small figure on the smooth sward – a small figure in a nightshirt, holding an open book, rising to his knees, his small face twisted with unbelievable pain. But the next moment the canvas shrivelled in the intense heat, the flames licked across, flared up, and the painting was consumed with a crackling roar – and a small high-pitched sound that might have been a desperately thin bubbling scream of mortal agony.

Then again, it might not.

III

Puckham's End Wood

If you leave Cheltenham by the road pointing east, proceed for about three miles and then turn north, you will enter a very rural area where the wolds spread wide and the houses are exceedingly few-and-far-between, and very well hidden. The populace is also none-too-easily visible and you might perhaps be forgiven for imagining that you are the only human being for miles around. There is plenty of animal life, and many birds, and there are indications that land cultivation and crop production goes on. But you could easily fancy that it all happens by remote control – which, of course, is very far from true.

If, undaunted by your solitude, you journey on, for possibly another three or four miles, you arrive at a valley wherein lurks a compact and dense area of woodland. The trees composing this woodland are, in the main, deciduous – oaks, planes, sycamores, maples and ash – with thick bracken and tangled undergrowth betwixt and between. On the upper slopes the soil is more sandy and here flourishes the stately beech and the graceful silver birch.

In summer the woodland is well populated, not only by our furred and feathered friends but by variegated specimens of humanity – to wit, hikers, picnickers, joggers, strollers, lovers and even, I regret to say, the occasional vandal. Blackberries are there for the picking (in the appropriate season); bluebells carpet the forest floor between the massive boles: innumerable birds throng the foliage and fill the air with song. But in winter the woodland

41

is rarely visited. A sharp bitter wind blows from the hills down through the valley and between the stark and leafless branches, whilst the gloomy spaces between the dark trees are filled with the cold empty rattle of dead leaves and the eerie dripping silence that accompanies the death of autumn.

This is Puckham's End Wood.

If you have ever wondered, as I have, if there ever was someone called Puckham who lived hereabouts, and – if there was – who was he and what was his 'end', then you will be interested in my next tale.

Recently I received a letter from a Mrs Craig, matron of the Westlands Nursing Home in Greville Road. It read:

> 'Forgive me for writing to you, but a friend of mine told me you were interested in strange stories concerning this town and its environs. We have in this Home an old man – a Mr Reynolds – who has a very interesting story to tell. How true it is I don't know, but if you care to come here he will willingly relate it to you, and you will then be able to judge for yourself. However, I would advise you to come as soon as possible: he is over ninety and has not long to live.'

I have to admit here and now that I did not relish the thought of visiting an old man on his death-bed (which, from what Mrs Craig had written, I assumed was the case), but her use of the word 'willingly' to describe the way in which he would accede to my request spurred me on.

I was surprised and relieved to find him looking a lot less like a corpse than I had feared. He was very thin – almost emaciated – and his bony hands were like claws as they clutched at the bedclothes, but his sunken cheeks had plenty of colour and his eyes in their deep sockets were bright as small buttons.

"Don't get many callers, I don't," he asserted, in a weak but clear voice after I had shaken his meagre fingers and taken a seat by his bed. "Well, y'see, I've outlived all me pals, haven't I . . .

and most of me family too. But you've 'eard all about that from 'er, I shouldn't wonder."

' 'Er', presumably, was Mrs Craig, and I had to confess to him that she had already told me he was a widower, his wife having died more than forty years before, and both his sons were dead, and his only brother likewise. His next-of-kin appeared to be a grandson living up north somewhere – Whitby, I think.

"What about your grandson?" I asked. "Doesn't he come to see you?"

"Him!" he said, with a world of scorn in his voice. "He don't never think of me. All he thinks of is motorbikes and girls. Not that I got anythin' agin the lassies, mind you. I was reckoned to be a bit of a spark in me day, and you can lay to that." His white eyebrows went up and down busily and he nodded. "Aye, reckon I've had me moments, I have. Had me moments, true enough."

"I'm sure you have," I responded soothingly.

We chatted for a while, but I've always found myself a bit out of my depth when talking to the bedridden, and in any case the matron had warned me not to overtax his strength. So after about ten minutes I tackled him about the 'very interesting story' Mrs Craig had mentioned in her letter. In reply he gave me a stare.

"Thought you 'adn't come here jist to give an old man a bit of company," he said, albeit without rancour.

"I'm sorry," I said at once. "I admit to having an axe to grind. You will probably have guessed that it isn't my usual habit to visit folks in hospitals or nursing-homes. But you must blame Mrs Craig. She wrote to me about you, said that something strange had happened to you that would make a good story. I'm always on the lookout for such stories and so I felt I owed it to myself to come and see you. If you wish, I'll come and visit you on a regular basis, and even get some of my friends along to chat with you: it's the least I can do in return."

But he only grinned faintly and lifted a bony hand as though to stop me saying anything more.

"I was only joshing," he said. "Glad of anyone's company these days." He sighed, his hollow chest rising and falling jerkily, then he fastened his eyes on my face. "So you wants to 'ear all about it, eh? You wants to 'ear what 'appened to me in Puckham's End Wood, is that it?"

"I do indeed," I responded, excitement burgeoning inside me. "So that's where it was! Certainly I'd love to hear it – very much so. Are you prepared to tell me?"

He nodded and for a long moment lay motionless, his emaciated body a slender ridge under the bedclothes. I assumed he was collecting his thoughts.

"It were a bit o' a step out of town in them days," he said at last. "Place 'as grown like billy-o since the war. And that's when it 'appened, y'see: after the war."

"As recently as that?" I experienced a twinge of disappointment, as though anything that happened only fifty or so years back could not possibly be as interesting as earlier events.

"Recent?" he said. "Nigh on eighty year ago?"

"Oh, you mean the First World War – 1914-1918!" I exclaimed.

" 'Course that's the one I meant," he responded almost scornfully. "A sight too old for the other, I was. Home Guard and fire-watching, that's all they said I was good for in that one. No, no: the first one. I was in the Navy three years, got blew up once, invalided out in '17, came inland to live. Fed up with the sea. It weren't a bad little place 'ere then. Too big now, o' course: too many people, too much traffic. The world's got a sight too crowded for the likes o' me."

He paused, as though reviewing in his mind the passing of the past.

"Come 1920 or thereabouts I was doing OK, working for a chap as made barrels for the brewery in town. You knows our brewery, I suppose? Back o' the 'igh street. Closed down now though: more's the pity. Buggers turned to making their own barrels after the war, which meant that the bloke what I worked for 'ad no job, and so neither 'ad I. But that's all water under the bridge now, I reckon. Up to then I was in work, labouring by day and courting by night." A surprisingly lecherous grin spread over his wrinkled countenance and he glanced slyly at me. "I s'pose you think we old'uns never 'ad no fun when we was young, eh?"

Ignoring my hasty protests, he went on: "Don't you believe it! We
'ad our moments, I can tell you. I 'ad me fair share and p'raps a
bit over, you might say. "He gave a throaty but decidedly
libidinous chuckle. "But I ain't going to tell you what me and
Charlotte – ah, that were her name right enough: Charlotte – got
up to down in Puckham's End Wood. Don't you believe 'em
when they tells you all the girls in them days were shy and didn't
know what to do with what nature give 'em. Some of 'em knew
what was what, and you can lay to that. Charlotte did! Pretty as a
picture, long black hair down to her waist, big dark eyes, and as
neat a body as any lad feeling 'is oats could ever hope to lay 'is
'ands on. And she weren't backward in coming forward, as you
might say. The wood was far enough away from the town in them
days – *and* it 'ad the reputation for being 'aunted, though no one
knew why. So me and Charlotte 'ad it to ourselves – no one about
to fix their nasty peeping-tom eyes on what we was up to. And
what we was up to was nobody's business, I can tell you. She
thought naught of stripping herself bare-arsed: in them days,
when to see a girl in 'er shirt was nothing short of a miracle!
And . . . and she . . . she used to . . ."

Mercifully for my blushes, words failed him at this point and
he lay still, clearly reminiscing to himself about his days of wine
and roses, whilst a seraphic smile played about his wrinkled
features. I hoped his heart would stand the strain of his memories
and eventually I said, "Er . . . what exactly *was* this happening
that took place there?"

"Oh – that," he said, coming to the surface of his reverie.
"Well, it all started one night. Must have been around midnight, I
reckons. Can't remember zactly what we was a-doing – and
wouldn't let on if I could – but suddenly we was interrupted by a
sort of low sobbing. We was in a clearing nigh-on near the middle
of the wood and it was dark as the inside of your hat, supposing
you wore one, which I didn't, nor nothing else either." And he
cackled wheezily. "We jumped yards, I can tell you, and she
clutched hold of me and we was still quivering when it come
again – a low sobbing moan, not far from where we was. Then –
a bit later – what sounded like a woman a-sobbing: 'No, no, no –

oh my Gord, no!' Charlotte gasped, 'Bill, what's that?' Me name's Bill, by the way. 'Dunno,' I said, 'sounds like someone in trouble.' She said, 'Let's go, Bill: let's get away from here.' Well, I have to admit I was a mite scared, but I was a well-plucked young'un in them days and, after we'd got dressed (and heard some more horrible moaning), I remembered a box of lucifers what I had in me pocket. Charlotte was a-pulling at me, begging me to take her away from there, but I got out the lucifers and struck one. And then – well, I thought I saw something."

"Like what?"

"Couldn't rightly say. It were white – and kind of – shimmering. Not upright, mind you: it were flat – and hovering above the ground weird-like – as much as three feet up, I reckons. It looked a bit like a – a corpse! It didn't look like nothing natural. Suddenly an 'orrible gurgling scream came from it, and me lucifer went out.

"Well, that put the kybosh on it, as you might say. Charlotte gave a sort of whimper and took to her heels. Of course, I had to follow her, didn't I, and we shot out of that wood like the devil hisself was at our heels, and who's to say he wasn't? Anyways, we didn't stop till we was on the main road."

I stared at him, not sure whether to believe him or not.

"What was it then?" I asked.

He shook his head wearily, as though exhausted by his talking.

"Dunno. No idea, son – no idea at all."

"Did it happen again?"

"Oh aye. Next night in fact."

"You didn't go there the following night again?" I said, deeply impressed.

"That I did. Only *this* time my mates Tom and Eric was with me. We was all good mates, we was. Tom worked for the same chap as what I did, and Eric laboured for the brewery. We met the next evening in the Coach and 'orses and I told 'em what 'ad 'appened. They didn't believe me – no more than what you don't, son – and so I gave 'em a challenge, to come with me that night and see if it 'appened again."

"And did they?"

46

"They did."

"And did it?"

"Did it what, son?"

"Happen again."

"Oh aye."

"Exactly the same thing?"

He shook his head.

"No. There was changes. Now hold on, son: let me tell it my way, eh? We got there afore midnight and hid ourselves in a clump of bushes near where Charlotte and me 'ad 'ad our bit of fun the night before. I took along a lantern just in case – not lit, mind – and some lucifers. Tom 'ad a thick walking stick belonging to 'is pa, and Eric 'ad a knife what his poacher mate 'ad given to 'im. And, since we all 'ad 'earty appetites, we took along some bread and cheese and beer. We sat there in the dark, all quiet-like, and waited."

Once again Bill ceased to talk, lay back and closed his eyes as though worn out.

I said, "Should I come back and hear the rest another day?"

"No, no. Don't worry about me son, I'll be all right." He opened his eyes and looked at me steadily. "I might not be 'ere tomorrow, see."

"Rubbish!" I said firmly, but without a lot of conviction.

He shook his head.

"I've had me innings – longer than most. Time to get back to the pavilion. Did I tell you I used to play for Cheltenham Town? First team, too. Ah, them were the days all right."

"Cricket?"

"Aye. Allus wanted to play first class, but I weren't good enough, see." He was silent for a moment, then asked, "Where was I?" I reminded him and he gave a nod. "Oh aye, I remembers. Well, the three of us waited, in the dark and the quiet. It weren't all dark, mind you: there was a little bitty moon we could see through the branches above our 'eads. It were dry and mild, and the forest smelt kind've earthy, and we could 'ear birds chirruping sleepily and animals rustling around us.

"Suddenly it 'appened. Another of them low sobbing moans –

just like the night before. And not far away, neither." He chuckled. "I remembers, just like it were yesterday, the looks on me mates' faces. Then it comes again, followed by an 'orrible scream. Tom was all for getting out and made no bones about it, but Eric 'ad more spunk. 'There's summat mighty wrong 'ere,' he said. 'It's a woman and she's in trouble.' And 'e picked up the lantern, lit it, and made off towards the noises. Well, I wasn't going to be left out and so I followed 'im, and Tom came too. We went through the trees, not caring what sort of noise we was making. Then we 'eard another moan, and another scream, this time right by us! Eric held up the lantern and I could see 'is face was white. And I reckons ours was as well. For a moment we could see nothing, but a bit later Tom gave a great cry. 'There . . . over there . . . what is it?' And 'is voice was 'oarse and kind've trembly-like."

The old man stopped again and his mouth quivered.

"And what was it?" I prompted, burning with curiosity.

His thin chest rose and fell in a sigh and he shook his head.

"Summat white," he said at last. "Wasn't all that clear – sort of blurred, know what I mean? – sort of misty-like, and changing, almost as though it were . . . trying to come clearer and not making it. A white shape, not flat this time but upright . . . and hanging . . . high up, way above our 'eads . . . hanging and swaying. It were right 'orrible," he finished, unable to put his remembrance of the dreadful moment into the right words. He lay with his eyes closed and I waited patiently, but he didn't stir and eventually I touched him on the shoulder.

"What happened next?" I asked gently.

He opened his eyes. "We stood sort of numb, just watching, too frit to move, y'see. Then the white shape shimmered and just seemed to fade away until there was nothing left to see – nothing at all.

"That was when Tom decided 'e'd 'ad enough. He gave a sort of gasp, turned and took to 'is heels, as fast as 'e could. Well, me and Eric 'ad to follow him, didn't we? We wasn't going to stay there on our own. We both galloped out of the wood, just as me and Charlotte 'ad done the night before, and we didn't go back neither."

Once more he ceased speaking and rested his head on the pillow. For the second time I suggested that I come back another day, but he still wouldn't hear of it.

"Nearly finished me story now," he said with a weak grin. "You wants to 'ear the rest, I s'pose?"

"Of course I do, Bill."

He nodded. "Bide your time then, son, bide your time." He lay, clearly gathering his strength, then he went on, "It 'appened one more time, y'see."

"You went there again?" I asked in surprise.

"We did. You see, here's the way of it. Tom was a Roman Catholic. Well, he 'ad a sort of brainstorm and went and confessed to 'is priest. Silly beggar! Upshot was that this priest – fellow called Belding, if I remembers right – wanted to do a – what do you call it? – exorcism – in the wood where we seen the white shape. It was 'is idea that there was an unhappy spirit in there and it wanted laying to rest like. Local police sergeant – name of Johnson – got to hear of it and next thing I know there's a sort of expedition up there that same night. Well, of course, Tom 'ad to go along – being it were 'im what confessed – and 'e got permission for me and Eric to go along as well. It were only right, after all.

"So there we all were, just after midnight, crouched down in the bushes where it 'ad 'appened before. Belding 'ad a few things with 'im – big silver crucifix, Bible, that sort of thing – and Johnson had a bull's-eye lantern and 'is truncheon. Eric and me had lanterns and sticks. Once again it were all dark and quiet as the grave. Plenty of animals and birds rustling in the undergrowth, but I reckons we were the only 'uman beings for miles around. I remembers we 'ad an owl 'oot at us once or twice, made us all jump – except Johnson, but 'e was in the Force, wasn't 'e, and didn't ought to jump.

"Well, to cut a long story short, it started to 'appen around 1am, straight away, no warning. An 'orrible scream, not far away: Johnson reckoned about fifty yards. It was the worst I'd 'eard up till then, like a soul in terrible torment. Strangely enough,

Johnson took it to 'eart more'n we did: well, we'd 'eard summat like it afore, 'adn't we? 'God's truth!' he said shakily. 'What the 'elf was that?' Belding told him off for taking the Lord's name in vain and Johnson said 'e was sorry. Then it 'appened again, another scream, worser than the first: then another, even more 'orrible. Belding 'ad 'is 'ead in 'is 'ands, and he was praying-like, under his breath. We didn't feel too good about the screams: fair turned my blood cold, they did, and I reckons Eric felt the same. But then Johnson speaks up. 'That's no damned spirit,' 'e said out loud. 'That's a woman's voice and she wants 'elp.' He lit 'is lantern, sprang to 'is feet and held the lantern up aloft. The light fell on a white shape, just like we saw before, all faint and shimmering, ghostly, like it 'adn't come through proper. It was high in the air, hanging, and sort of bent. Eric reckoned afterwards it was all of ten feet up. Then – all of a sudden – we 'eard a rattle of chains. The white shape fell, almost to the ground, followed by an outburst of the worst screaming what you've never 'eard in all your life."

The old man lay back exhausted, breathing shallowly. Once more I offered to leave and come back another day but, as before, he shook his head.

"I'm nigh on done now," he said. (I hoped he meant his story, not his life.) "Be patient, son. That's the trouble with the world today: everyone's in too much of a blinking hurry." He found the strength to tap my arm with a heavy finger. "Learn to take it easy, that's my advice. Don't be in such a dad-blamed hurry about everything. Take it slow and easy, like what I did. And I ain't done so bad, have I?"

He lay still a few minutes more, then resumed his story.

"Belding muttered, 'Dear God, there is a spirit here what needs succour and rest.' He turned to Johnson. 'Come with me, sergeant,' he said, 'I've a job to do. You lads stay here.' Johnson squared his jaw and together the two men walked slowly towards the white shape what had been rising and falling whilst we talked, plus the screams, which were getting worse. Being good lads, we did as we was told, and we watched Johnson hold his lantern aloft, and Belding holding the great silver cross over his head and muttering all sorts of things – prayers, incantations, whatever – but we couldn't hear a word of it, o' course. This went on for quite a while, and gradually the screams got fainter and fainter, and the white shape shimmered and got sort of transparent, and after a while there was nothing left, only a sort of distant sobbing noise. Then that stopped and it was silence from then on.

"We all waited quite a bit more, but nothing happened after that, so we packed up and came away."

He drew a deep breath, was quiet for a while, then added, "And that's about the size of it, son. That priest must have hit on what was needed, 'cos we went again the next night and there was nothing – nothing at all. And from then on there weren't no more disturbances in that place. The hauntings had finished."

He lay still, hardly breathing, his eyes closed, so silent and so lifeless that I thought he'd gone.

"Mr Reynolds . . . " I ventured.

"Bill," he said almost inaudibly. "The name's Bill."

"Bill then," I said. "Is that it?"

He nodded.

"Didn't you ever find out why the wood was haunted?"

"No. We wasn't so keen on finding out answers to things in them days, nor did we have the time. And anyways the priest said we shouldn't. 'Whatever it was is laid to rest,' he said. 'Leave it be, there's good lads.' And so we did."

Soon after that I took my departure, but I was in no mood to emulate the absence of natural curiosity that had apparently possessed the principal participants in the drama. I wanted some answers. Unfortunately I was hampered by a total lack of clues, and was consequently at a loss to know where to start. In the end I decided to have a look at the 'scene of the crime', but this did not help in the least. There may have been a substantial wood there at one time, but now it was smaller and surrounded by fields. I went as far as to look at a few old maps, dating back to the mid 1800s, but all this proved was that the location, and the name, had been in existence for well over a century.

I was stumped as to what to do next. I talked the matter over with a few friends and one of them – in a humorous mood – put me onto my next phase of investigation.

"Puckham's End Wood?" he said. "Perhaps you ought to find out who this bloke Puckham was, and what exactly his horrible end was."

The very next day I paid a visit to several parish churches and went through the records. I found quite a few Puckhams – obviously a fairly common name in the area – but not one of them, as far as I could ascertain, came to a sticky end in a wood. Then I looked up all the Puckhams in the local telephone directory. There were dozens listed, but only four in Cheltenham. I telephoned them, and in one instance went to see them, but – although I received the utmost courtesy and co-operation – I learned nothing new.

Once again my quest seemed to have come to an end, and in desperation I sought advice from members of the local history society. Again, everyone concerned was most helpful, but it turned out that there was nothing in any of the books or documents relating to the town or its environs which gave me any clues.

To cut a long story short, I was on the point of giving up when a chance remark by a friend of mine whilst we were supping pints at the Cock & Bull put me on a new scent. He is, I regret to say, of a somewhat libidinous turn of mind and, when I'd described to him the phenomena Bill Reynolds had witnessed back in 1920, he gave an earthy chuckle.

"Sounds like a bit of an orgy to me," he said.

"Orgy!" I exclaimed. "How do you make that out? You've got a mind like a sewer."

"Probably, but that's not the point. What was it his pals saw? White shapes – vertical, horizontal, going up and down. Sounds to me like one gigantic joyous orgy. They had 'em in the old days, depend on it. And those sobbing moans and horrible screams! Ecstasy, me old fruit, not pain. Or perhaps a bit of both. If you're looking for violent emotion to persist through the ages, and come out much later, you really don't have to look any further."

"Rubbish! Tell me why it just happened to come out, as you put it, when Reynolds and his girl were there."

"Easy. Because they were at the same game. Probably caused some kind of sympathetic reaction which brought out what you might call the psychic residue that had been lying dormant for years. That's the answer, depend on it." He stared into his pint, thoughtfully. "You never know, it might have been a meeting of the local coven. These witches knew a thing or two: used to get up to some right old capers, I believe. Porn wasn't invented in the twentieth century, old lad. Good thing old Matt Hopkins wasn't around at the time."

"Who?"

"Matthew Hopkins. They called him the Witch-finder. Never heard of him? He was a sort of witch detector – operated out of some town in Essex, I think. Mind you, this was hundreds of years ago – and I don't believe he was ever down this way."

It was a slender chance, but I seized on it. I went to the local library and investigated. And for the first time I learned all about the notorious Matthew Hopkins, Witchfinder extraordinary.

My friend had been right when he said it was hundreds of years ago. Hopkins appears to have come in to the public eye around 1645, and retired out of it only some 18 months later. Yet in that incredibly short space of time he is alleged to have been responsible for the detection and conviction of some hundreds of so-called witches – of whom over 200 were sentenced to death and the sentence carried out in an unbelievably barbarous fashion.

Needless to say, that kind of productivity was not possible single-handed. Hopkins had help – a partner named John Stearne, as well as assistant witch-prickers Mary Phillips and Edward Parsley. Nevertheless, the fees he received (and no doubt these were part of his raison d'être – the others being an obsessional puritanism and an overwhelming desire for personal power) were sufficient to enable him to pay his team and pocket some very handsome profits. One instance of the scale of his income need only be given: one authority states that a single journey to Stowmarket in Suffolk for the purposes of giving evidence at a trial netted him £23 – equivalent to something like 2 years' salary for the average wage-earner of that day.

Matthew Hopkins was a product of his time. The struggle

between the Cavaliers and the Roundheads was hotting up; the counties of Essex, Suffolk, Norfolk and Bedfordshire in particular were a-boil with the new Protestantism, and the time was ripe for a person of strong ambition and even stronger stomach to play the part of demagogue. Hopkins, whose origins are obscure, is thought to have been born in Suffolk, the son of a minister. He became a little-known lawyer and, after failing to make the grade in Ipswich, he moved to Manningtree in Essex. It was here that he stepped out of the ruck of extras to become the leading actor in what turned out to be a horror play. He came into prominence by denouncing one Elizabeth Clarke, a poor one-legged old woman, as a witch, and followed that up very swiftly with five others whom Clarke had named whilst under severe torture. Hopkins' success attracted John Stearne, who joined him, and between them these two increased the number of suspects to over thirty.

Matthew Hopkins took a section of the 'DEMONOLOGY' of King James 1st of Scotland (published 1597) as his biblical text. This concerned itself with the alleged invariable habit of all witches of keeping 'imps' or 'familiars'. Sometimes they were accused merely of suckling them; at other times it was alleged that the 'familiars' changed into devils and sexual intercourse took place. From then on, any woman (young or old) who kept a pet of almost any kind was deeply suspect. Cats, dogs, birds, rabbits: none was exempt from the clouds of suspicion that Hopkins and his cronies brewed and fermented. And, following the suspicions, fingers were pointed at the unfortunate owners of these pets and they were taken from their humble homes and subjected to torture. In some cases the infamous treatment was carried out in the victim's own home.

It is stated that, whilst Hopkins and his associates devised and developed certain techniques of torture to ensure that they extracted the confessions of guilt they required, they did not at any time resort to the barbarous and brutal methods practised on the Continent (mainly France and Germany). Nevertheless, the methods they were known to have employed proved highly efficacious. 'Swimming' (casting bound women into the village pond to see if they sank) was initially popular, but in 1645 a Parliamentary Commission ruled against this vile practice, and Hopkins was obliged to change to other ways and means. Since these involved such niceties as prevention of sleep, forced continuous walking, prolonged squatting cross-legged on a stool, and even starvation (all of which were permissible), confessions continued to come freely.

Charges varied from bewitching: to death through damage to property: injury to cattle: and to 'entertaining evil spirits' (these being the pets the poor harmless women kept). Since in those days all those accused of any kind of misdemeanour were adjudged guilty until proved innocent, convictions followed fast upon judgement, and death by hanging followed conviction.

Flushed with his successes at the Chelmsford County Sessions, Hopkins widened his field of endeavour. He was now rich, and employed a team of no less than six assistants. Having scoured Essex for victims, he moved his activities north-east to Norfolk and Suffolk, then extended his nefarious dealings to encompass the shires of Cambridge, Northampton, Hertford and Bedford, and a year later penetrated west, via Buckinghamshire and Oxfordshire into Gloucestershire. This latter county proved a particularly fertile hunting-ground for him and his followers, as it was well removed from the civilising influence of London, whilst outside the towns the inhabitants of the countryside were primitive, unlettered and much given to ancient superstitions.

By 1646 Hopkins was known and feared throughout the southern half of England as 'The Witchfinder General', and was reckoned to have caused the death of over 200 alleged witches – including a number of men. One of these, a seventy-year-old parson called John Lowes, was supposed to have covenanted with the Devil, bewitched cattle, and even caused the sinking of a ship off Harwich!

It was soon after this that Hopkins met his Waterloo. A clergyman of Huntingdon, by name John Gaule, resented Hopkins' methods, fearing that he might invade his own county. He began to preach against him with fire and fervour, and found many people in accord with his views. Hopkins counteracted with a pamphlet entitled 'Discovery of Witches', but this was denounced as 'sanctimonious hypocrisy'.

The final blow to Hopkins' career came when he was accused of extracting confessions by illicit means from a woman living in Winchcombe, Gloucestershire. The woman – a one-armed widow named Margaret Puckham – was accused of causing pestilence among cattle and sheep, working spells to prevent butter churning or beer brewing, and – in particular – bewitching to death the wife of a minister. She was alleged to have confessed to all these crimes after three days of 'treatment' by several members of Hopkins' team. But, unfortunately for them, someone talked. The local judges got to hear of the accusation of gross cruelty levelled at Hopkins and his associates, and all the miscreants were forced to flee the area. Hopkins himself returned to his home town of Manningtree and died of tuberculosis the following year. John Stearne retired to Bury St. Edmunds: the others disappeared from sight and were never heard of again.

You may imagine my elation when I read the name of Hopkins' last victim. Was this the origin and source of 'Puckham's End'? I investigated further, ending up at the British Museum Library, in London. Here, after much patient enquiry, and not a little help from the Chief Librarian and his willing assistants, I unearthed a publication describing the proceedings of a trial at the Gloucester County Assizes in 1646 relating to one Margaret Puckham of Syreford, near Cheltenham, in the county of Gloucestershire. An extract from the voluminous report will suffice to show the nature of the 'evidence' on which Hopkins and his crew based their accusations.

There dwelt within the Parish of Syreford, near Cheltenham, a certain parson, by name Thomas Searle, who lived with his wife Martha in a house adjacent to the village green. Martha's first husband, a farmer, had died some years previously, leaving her with a small farm. Eventually she had married again, taking Thomas Searle to husband.

One day Thomas was in the orchard, gathering apples, when Martha came to him in sore distress and did complain most bitterly that there was some curse laid upon the farm animals, in that the cows did naught but give green and stinking milk, the sheep would not eat and were growing very thin, and the hens were stumbling like drunkards and laying eggs with no yolks.

When he asked her why this was so, she averred that it was all the fault of 'yonder wicked and unnatural creature' who lived in a hut in a small wood nearby. This was one Margaret Puckham, a middle-aged widow, a buxom woman who had been known to grant her favours to many men in the village (and on whom Thomas Searle had more than once cast a secret and lascivious eye). Martha further deposed that she had seen said Margaret Puckham, at dead of night, arriving back at her hut through the air astride a besom, with a large black cat seated behind her: and that this had happened more than once.

Thomas then did ask his wife how she could have seen such occurrences at dead of night, when all was dark, but she remained defiant and repeated her accusations.

The next day Thomas Searle went to the hut in the wood, where he did confront the said Margaret Puckham with his wife's suspicions. The accused did become very angry and not only denied the allegations, but went on to state that Martha Searle was 'a wicked, wicked whore' who told lies, and she added that in her opinion he, the said Thomas Searle, was worthy of a better woman, and who else was she talking about but herself?

Thomas Searle hastily reminded her that he was not only married, but a member of the Church and so not amenable to her wiles. It was however some considerable time, so it is alleged, before he departed from the hut.

From then on his wife Martha did become sore afflicted and did take to her bed, and was subsequently laid low with an evil pestilential sickness which no one recognised and which even William Booth, famed healer of that parish, was not able to treat. And witnesses stated that within seven more days the unfortunate woman's soul had fled her body and this world, and no one knew the cause of her going. And Thomas Searle was exceeding sad for a while: but soon afterwards, so it is said, sought comfort in a place not far from his home, although this was no more than idle gossip and not something to be bruited abroad.

It is some measure of the suspicions attached to Hopkins and his team, and of the new enlightened attitude of the judges, that Margaret Puckham was found not guilty and acquitted of all charges.

I took the opportunity whilst at the British Museum Library to seek knowledge concerning the 'illicit means, as practised in certain foreign parts' by which the witch-prickers had extracted a confession from the unfortunate Margaret Puckham. To say that I was appalled by what I learned is to put it mildly. The barbaric cruelty that was inflicted on the unhappy victims, the total absence of any regard for human life or dignity, must surely make a mockery of the term 'the good old days'. Being English, I was not too displeased to find that such abominable behaviour was almost totally confined to Germany and France (and, to a lesser extent, Scotland) although we in England can find little satisfaction in reading about the so-called 'lesser' techniques used in this country.

It seems that, on the Continent, it was the custom in the fifteenth and sixteenth centuries to subject accused persons to hideous tortures which, traditionally, fell into three phases. The accused (generally a woman) was stripped naked, her clothing searched for the means of witchcraft which may have been secreted in them, and her body searched for Devil's marks, such as additional teats, moles, wens, birthmarks, etc. She was then bound with ropes, which were subsequently tightened gradually to increase the pain of bondage, and she was stretched on the rack or, failing this, a ladder could be utilised for the purpose. Whilst this exceedingly slow and agonising process was taking place, sharp instruments, occasionally heated to a red glow, were inserted under the fingernails and, regrettably, in other parts of the body.

If all this did not succeed in extracting a confession, the victim was revived and left overnight without food or water, to await the second stage. This consisted in the main of a fiendish operation known as *Strappado*, where the victim's arms were tied behind her back with a rope attached to a pulley fixed to the ceiling, by which means she was then hoisted upwards and left to hang in this grotesque manner for hours on end. At such times thumbscrews were often applied, not only to the fingers but also the toes, whilst sessions of flogging were also undertaken.

If this second session of diabolical treatment was not enough to secure a confession, the very next day the torturers proceeded to the third phase. This involved strappado again, but a more fiendish refinement of same, under which the victim was bound and hoisted to the ceiling in the manner already described, but then was suddenly – and without any warning – released to drop almost, but not quite, to the ground. This caused intense agony and sometimes complete dislocation of joints. Should this not prove efficacious, there were even more revolting practices which could be employed, such as the laceration of the victim's naked flesh with the severed claws of wild animals, total immersion in scalding baths, forced walking for days on end, and so on.

I may say here that, reading all about this seemingly incredible yet well-documented cruelty made me feel physically sick. I also began to appreciate that, if Margaret Puckham had been subjected to any or all of these bestial tortures, in the place now known as Puckham's End Wood, it was little wonder that this locality had retained what my friend called 'psychic residue' of the terrible ordeal and indescribable agony she had undergone. The only question that formed itself in my mind was why there had been only one known occasion when the replication of the torment suffered by this poor woman had been witnessed. Why had there been no reports of anything similar happening prior to the time Bill Reynolds and his paramour went to the wood for amorous dalliance in 1920? And why not subsequently? – unless the exorcism carried out by the priest had had due effect.

Hoping to find answers to these questions, I went back to the Westlands Nursing Home to see Bill Reynolds a second time. To my shocked surprise I learned that he was dead.

"Coronary thrombosis," said Mrs Craig in a matter-of-fact voice. "Yesterday morning. To be perfectly frank, we've been expecting it for some time. However, I'm glad to be able to report that he suffered little or no pain. Woke up, went to the toilet, came back to his bed, and died."

I was of course saddened to hear this news, not only because my story seemed to have suddenly acquired an abrupt and unhappy ending, but also because I had, in the one short visit, become quite attached to the old chap.

"I suppose he doesn't have any relations by the name Puckham, does he?" I asked as I prepared to leave.

She shook her head – then held up her hand. "Hold on. The name *does* sound familiar."

She opened a drawer in her desk and extracted a cardboard box. "These are his personal effects, found on him after he died. There were a number of very old papers, and this was one of them."

She passed me a document, yellowed with age, tattered and fragile. I opened it carefully. It was a marriage certificate, faded but still legible. It was a record of a marriage between William C. Reynolds, cooper's labourer, of Cheltenham, and Charlotte M. Puckham, spinster, of Winchcombe. It was dated 1921.

IV

Grange Walk

Grange Walk is a pleasant thoroughfare, typical of many residential roads throughout Cheltenham. It is reached by proceeding along the London Road, branching right at the Holy Apostles Church, going for some half-mile and then . . . well, the exact location need not be specified. It is a long road and ends up on the slopes of one of the hills surrounding the town. It is lined on both sides by a pleasing mixture of large well-established houses, plus a few blocks of flats that have been constructed, thank goodness, with at least some regard for their aesthetic appeal. The latter are relatively new: twenty years ago all the houses were owner-occupied.

Number 13 was one such.

Reading in the local paper of my interest in strange stories connected with the town, Mr J. Probert, superintendent of the Eastwood Institute (a mental hospital some miles out of town) sent me a sheaf of papers, which I found to consist of a score or more of foolscap filled with a pencilled scrawl that was difficult, although fortunately not impossible, to read.

The accompanying letter read as follows:

The enclosed MSS is by Mr Damien Sidley, a patient of ours who died a month ago from a choking fit during lunch. He has been a patient at this establishment ever since he was transferred from Broadmoor with severe cardiac problems. He was committed to

61

Broadmoor towards the end of 1976 after he had been tried, and found guilty, of murdering his wife.

When his room was cleared, the enclosed was found crammed behind a drawer of a tallboy. We knew he did writing – my staff provided him with the necessary materials – but he would never reveal what he was writing about, and we did not ask him about it, as both his illness and his mental state made it very difficult to communicate with him.

We endeavoured to trace relatives, but with little success. As far as is known, he had no issue and no siblings. We believe there is a cousin of sorts out in New Zealand, but so far he has not been traced. I have the permission of the solicitors acting on behalf of the estate to send the MSS to you, as I am sure you will find it to be of interest, if of doubtful credibility.

I did, Mr Probert, indeed I did.

I made some enquiries about Mr Damien Sidley, but found little to augment the information provided by Mr Probert. The subject of my researches had indeed been convicted of murdering his wife in 1976. It seems he battered her to death whilst in bed with her, on the first night of their sojourn in the house they had just bought. Although he was not called to give evidence, he made no secret of his motive: he averred that it had not been his wife in bed with him but a monster from the deepest pits of hell intent on his destruction and he had only acted in self-defence. Small wonder that the jury had been unanimous in declaring him guilty but insane!

Incidentally, I paid a visit to Grange Walk to have a look at No. 13 – with, I fear, the inevitable consequence. I found only a block of flats on the site: No. 13 had been demolished some years before.

And now for the MSS. Whether it is, as everyone believes, the figment of a madman's distorted imagination, or whether it is possible – just barely possible – that there is a grain of truth in it somewhere, I cannot say.

I leave you to be the judge.

The Manuscript

I knew there was something wrong with the house as soon as I stood outside on the pavement and looked at it.

Don't misunderstand me. I don't mean to imply that the house was structurally unsound, or that it suffered from dry rot, rising damp, a leaky roof or whatever. Maybe it did, but I was not an architect, surveyor or builder, nor even a reasonably competent handyman. I was merely a sales executive in a company marketing plastic kitchenware, looking for a bigger house for myself, my wife, and two dependent relatives.

No. I meant that there was something wrong with the house in the sense that . . . well, I'm not sure in what sense I meant it. Amongst other definitions of the word 'wrong', my dictionary gives 'undesirable'. And that fitted the house exactly. I felt the agent should have started his circular with the words: 'This undesirable residence . . . 'As soon as we got out of the car and looked up the driveway at the large double-gabled house, its mellow walls almost totally covered in Virginia Creeper, I felt an acute sense of foreboding.

"Well, now we're here let's go in," said my wife.

I did not move. Something was preventing me from doing as she suggested.

"Why are you hanging back?" she asked suspiciously.

"I don't know," I admitted with strict truthfulness.

"It's not the number, is it? Number thirteen?" She looked at me in a puzzled fashion, not knowing whether to laugh or be annoyed. "You're not superstitious."

"No. I've absolutely no objection to the number." I hesitated, then blurted out, "You remember me telling you about that nightmare I had a few weeks ago?" My throat was suddenly dry at the recollection. "I've got that same feeling again."

"You can't be serious," she said with understandable incredulity.

But I was. The nightmare in question had been very real and in consequence very frightening. I'm usually as level-headed as the next man, but to tell the truth it affected me like no other nightmare had ever done – and I've had my share.

As was usual with the vast majority of my dreams, the details were vague, my physical senses only dimly aware of my environment. In contrast, my emotional senses were acutely affected, although 'agitated' might be a more appropriate term.

I was inside a house. Without actually 'seeing' the walls, doors, ceilings and floors, this much I knew. I also 'knew' that it was an older type of house, and fairly large. Without knowing any facts, I 'felt' that it was a three-storey house, with large, lofty rooms, set in an extensive and grown-up garden.

I was on the ground floor, standing in a spacious wood-panelled hall that I can only describe as 'gloomy'. I was far from happy at being there, although I could not say why. I knew that I was alone, and that there was little light and no sound. In fact, the darkness was almost a positive 'entity', almost a presence. The silence too was not merely a lack of sound: it pressed upon the ear-drums and had a tingling quality, as though a mild electric discharge was taking place.

Anxious to leave this unsettling place, I strove to locate the way out. Instead, as often happens in dreams, I found myself floating up a stairway – a stairway that had a small landing half-way up, with a long window that I felt was of stained glass. I floated up further, to a landing as dark as the hall: yet I 'knew' that it was spacious and had many doors.

It was then that the feeling of disquiet increased. No cause – visible or audible – was present, yet I experienced an access of fear. I shook from head to foot; my heart thumped like a steam-hammer; my tongue clove to the dry roof of my mouth; the hair at the back of my neck prickled. Whatever the origin – man or beast, mental or physical, natural or unnatural – it was radiating waves of animosity, and they were directed at me. The source was not on the landing, but in one of the rooms.

Once again I tried to escape but, as before, I found myself moving inexorably towards a door, a door with carved panels of dark oak and a large brass doorknob that, despite my desperate struggles, I grasped and turned. I knew that beyond that door lay the source of the evil that was coming at me in waves, yet the door opened and I entered the room.

Now I was completely exposed to those searing currents of malignancy. The room was dark, but I knew it was large and oak-panelled. I also knew that within its confines lurked the origin of the shuddersome breakers of hate that flowed at and around me with incontestable malevolence. Despite this, I was propelled into the room, to face whatever might befall. The door shut behind me, the assault upon my senses and my sanity was redoubled . . . overwhelming . . . drowning . . .

I woke up at that moment – screaming.

The light went on and I slowly realised that I was in my own bed, in my own house, and my wife was leaning over me, hair falling over her eyes.

"Wake up, darling. You've been shrieking your head off. Whatever were you dreaming about, for goodness sake?"

I lay breathing quickly, drenched in sweat, still fearful yet conscious of the shadows of dread fading from my mind and from my body. Gradually my heart ceased to race. I drew a deep rasping breath.

"I – I don't know. I was in a room, in a strange house. There was – something in the room – something so horrible that – "

I shivered anew, recalling vividly the terror that had gripped me.

"It's looking at all these houses these past few weeks," she said sympathetically. "The sooner we get settled the better. Are you all right now?"

"Yes. As you said, I was dreaming. You can go back to sleep now."

"Well, thank you, darling."

She switched off the light, wriggled back down into the bed and, as was her usual wont, was fast asleep in seconds. But I lay awake for a long time, every now and then shivering as remembrance of the ordeal returned to haunt me. It was hours before I drifted off into an uneasy sleep.

That was some three weeks ago. In between now and then I had not been troubled similarly and in fact had almost forgotten that awful sensation of helpless terror that had seemed so real at the time. But now, standing at the entrance to the driveway of

13 Grange Walk, I felt the first faint stirrings of the same dread.

"Ridiculous, I know," I remarked, striving to keep it light. "Let's forget it, shall we? Do you like the look of the place?"

"Lovely. But it's a bit old, isn't it?" She referred to the agent's circular. "Erected in 1892. Still, they built them well in those days, didn't they? How do you feel about buying an older house?"

"I don't mind, as long as it's sound. We shall need a surveyor's report, of course."

"Let's go in."

A woman answered the doorbell. She was a Mrs Lock, in her early forties (I judged), wearing a well-filled sweater and a skirt shorter than I felt her age warranted. She ushered us into the hall, and immediately my heart went cold and once again I felt a prickling at the back of my neck. The hall was large, and oak-panelled, two narrow windows letting in so little light that it was quite gloomy, especially in comparison with the sunshine outside. I didn't know what to think or do – it could so easily have been the hall in my nightmare!

My wife touched my arm.

"Dear, Mrs Lock is talking to you."

"Oh – sorry!" I exclaimed, jerking myself back to normality. "I was miles away. You were saying . . ?"

"Just that my husband died three years ago, my youngest daughter a year ago, and my other two children have grown up and moved away, so the house is far too big for me now," she said. "Do you have much of a family?"

"No children," I replied. "But we have a couple of dependent relatives, so we shall need plenty of room."

"I think this house may well suit you down to the ground," she said. "It's on three floors. There are four living-rooms downstairs, three bedrooms and two bathrooms on the first floor, and two more bedrooms on the second floor. There is also a large fully-boarded and lit loft which could easily be converted into a sixth bedroom. Now, let me show you round."

I must admit I didn't pay too much attention to Mrs Lock's sales talk as she took us on a tour of the ground floor accommodation. I was still apprehensive – a feeling that seemed to be an echo, however slight, of the overwhelming fear that I had experienced in my dream. As we visited each of the downstairs rooms, I noted that they were all large and lofty. My practical side observed that the standard of decor and maintenance appeared to be high and, despite my anxiety, I began to be aware of a suspicion that this house might be just what we wanted.

The anxiety remained static downstairs, but increased sharply as Mrs Lock led us up the stairs. The stairway was oak-panelled like the hall, and halfway up there was a small landing with a tall window. My wife remarked on the attractive effect produced by the sun's rays shining through the stained glass: I was conscious only of my heart beating fast as I realised this was the stairway I had dreamed about. I felt I turned pale, but the two women did not appear to notice and went up to the main landing, chatting together quite happily. I was steeling myself to follow them when my wife looked down at me from over the balustrade. It was gloomy up there and I started violently, seeing only a dark shape and a pale visage and fancying that some horrible monster was glaring down at me. But then she spoke.

"Aren't you coming up?"

I forced myself to join her and Mrs Lock on the landing and the latter proceeded to show us the bedrooms. As we approached what she termed 'the master bedroom' my apprehension increased until my stomach was painfully knotted. The door had carved oak panels and a large brass doorknob. Once more it was like my nightmare and I could not for the life of me grasp that doorknob. Fortunately Mrs Lock performed that function without qualms and my wife followed her into the room. It looked like a normal room and when Sandra glanced round at me I drew a deep breath and went in.

The room was spacious and the walls oak-panelled. The sense of horror was now suffocating, yet there was no apparent reason for it. The room had two side windows which would have let in plenty of light but for the Virginia Creeper obscuring most of the glass.

"I am going to have that stuff trimmed back," said Mrs Lock, seeing our eyes on the windows. "I usually get a man in to do it about twice a year."

There was a large old-fashioned fireplace, blocked off with what looked like hardboard covered in wallpaper, and fronted by a formidable and thoroughly modern electric fire. There were two capacious cupboards with double doors. The furniture was modern and the carpet bright. There seemed to be no reason whatsoever for the atmosphere that I encountered in the room, but it was affecting me so much that Sandra saw it.

"Are you all right?" she asked. "You look a bit pale."

"I'm OK," I lied. I tried to pull myself together. "Let's see the rest of the house."

To my great relief we left the 'master bedroom', whereupon my apprehension abated somewhat. We viewed the other rooms on that floor and then climbed to the top storey. I noticed, almost with detachment, that the remainder of the house had no effect on me. And when we surveyed the extensive garden, and inspected the garage, my troubles well-nigh vanished. There was no doubt about it: whatever was the source of my inexplicable fears, it lurked in that main bedroom.

When we had quitted the Grange and were driving home, I dreaded the thought that Sandra was going to ask me what I thought of the house, and sure enough she did. I didn't know what to reply, so countered by asking, "What did *you* think of it?"

"As far as I can see, it's ideal," she answered. "It's got everything we need. But I could tell you were unhappy about it. Was it something to do with that nightmare you told me about?"

"You'll think I've gone potty. But, if you really want the truth, that house was the exact counterpart to the one in my dreams. Everything I felt in that dream – the horror, the apprehension, the dread – came right back to me: especially when I was in the master bedroom."

"That big bedroom? Why, that was the nicest room in the house. It would suit us to a 'T', seeing that we like plenty of space."

"I couldn't agree more. In fact I know damn well the house is just what we've been looking for. Even the price is right. If the house is sound, there is absolutely *no* reason why we shouldn't take the plunge."

"But . . ?"

I shrugged. "What can I say? I felt terrible in that bedroom – God knows why. Perhaps it's my health. I may have been overdoing it at the office lately. I don't know. Perhaps it won't happen again. I'd be stupid to let such an opportunity pass by for such a flimsy reason . . . wouldn't I?"

Sandra was silent for a while. Then she said, "It is ideal, I agree. I must admit I quite fell in love with it. The right size, the right position, the right price. It needs virtually nothing done to it. But well, it'd be madness to take it if you're going to be unhappy living there."

I could tell from her tone of voice that, whilst she was trying hard to be reasonable and sympathetic, nevertheless the germs of disappointment were breeding inside her. And I couldn't blame her. Whatever my 'feelings' were, they were only that: there was no logical basis for them.

"It's not merely a question of being unhappy," I said, conscious that I was being forced into a corner from which the only avenue of escape was one I was not going to like.

"What is it a question of then?" she asked levelly.

"It's not easy to explain," I said in an aggrieved voice. "Whilst I was in that house, I experienced a feeling of sheer hostility, animosity, vindictiveness – call it what you like – that was directed at me. Oh, this is ridiculous!" I exclaimed, becoming more and more annoyed. "You'll be ringing the local loony-bin and having me carted away any minute now."

My wife made no reply and her silence drove me to rashness.

"Look, I'll tell you what I'm willing to do. We'll get a surveyor's report on the house. And – just to satisfy myself – I'll make some enquiries concerning its previous history. If the first is OK, and the second produces nothing unusual, we'll go ahead and buy it. How does that suit you?"

"It suits me," she responded. "But does it suit you?"

"It's going to have to," I replied with more firmness than I felt. The survey was commissioned, but it would be a fortnight before it could be carried out. I spent that time trying to trace the history of 13 Grange Walk. This proved an interesting exercise, produced some intriguing facts, and caused some fanciful speculation, but I ended up with little to reassure me. The Locks had lived in the house for fifteen years and in that time had experienced nothing abnormal. However, I was cynical enough to assume that people trying to sell their house were not likely to divulge anything that might deter prospective purchasers. I ventured to ask Mrs Lock how her husband had died, wondering if this might have a bearing on the matter, but was informed that he had suffered a heart attack whilst working in the garage and had died three days later in hospital. The attack was thought to have been caused by stress and pressure of business. It was my wife who put to her the delicate question of her third child, and she succeeded in eliciting the information that she had died falling off a swing in the back garden, breaking her neck in the process. Other than these points, Mrs Lock had nothing to offer, although she was able to remember the name of the previous occupier – a Colonel Pemberton.

I then went to the estate agent, but he had nothing to add. He did however refer me to another agent in the town, saying that it was this firm that had handled the transfer of the property to the Locks fifteen years before. I went to see this second agent – a Mr Holmes (a not inappropriate name, I thought irreverently) – and, after I had jogged his memory, he looked up his records. The house had come upon the market suddenly, due to the death of Colonel Pemberton. The Locks, with three young children and the necessary finance (Mr Lock having recently obtained a senior position with an engineering firm in an adjacent town) had snapped it up. The colonel had been a childless widower at the time of his death, his wife having died soon after the end of the war, and the house had been left to a nephew living in America who had promptly arranged to have it sold and the proceeds remitted to him in the States.

"And that's about all I can tell you," he concluded.

"How long had the colonel been living there?"

"Since just after the war. He'd been with the army in India and when the war ended he retired and returned to England to live with his wife. Unfortunately she died a year later. Tragic business."

"Why would a childless couple need such a large house?" I wondered.

"Staff," replied Mr Holmes laconically. "I seem to remember there were at least two servants – Indians – to deal with when the colonel died. I believe, in fact, they went back to their native country."

That indeed was all he could tell me. I had to go elsewhere for the rest: firstly to the deeds, from which I learned that the previous owner had been a Dr Victor Boorman and he had lived in the house until 1939, after which it appeared to have remained empty until taken over by Colonel Pemberton in 1946. I was at first unable to glean any information concerning the doctor, but after a great deal of diligent enquiry I tracked down an older citizen of the town who had not only been a resident between the wars but who had some knowledge of the house itself. The man in question was a Mr Charles Benbow and I traced him to an old people's home in Duke Street. He had lived near Grange Walk between the wars and remembered the doctor. Apparently the latter had been of German origin and had practised medicine, specialising in several somewhat esoteric disciplines, one of which had been thought to be mesmerism; he had also run the house as a nursing home.

As was often the case with foreigners in English towns before the war, stories had sprung up regarding his (alleged) activities. One or two patients had died at the house and, although their deaths had been certified as being due to natural causes, mud had been thrown and some had stuck. Mr Benbow also recalled that the doctor had frequently travelled abroad on long trips, on occasions returning with unusual mementoes of his travels, the exact nature of which remained obscure.

Dr Boorman had been found dead in bed one morning, shortly after the outbreak of war in 1939. Once again death was found to be due to natural causes, but there had been, somewhat naturally, a strong anti-German feeling in the town and some whispered that he had been 'disposed of', by person or persons unknown. Others hinted darkly that his demise had been a form of retribution for certain sins committed during his lifetime, although neither the sins nor the murderers were named.

The house had remained empty throughout the war and, as is often the case with old houses left vacant for long periods, rumours of hauntings had begun to circulate. In 1942 a couple of tramps had been found dead inside the house, and after that people began to give the place a wide berth.

Then, in 1946, Colonel Pemberton had arrived home from India, scoffed at the stories, purchased the house, had it thoroughly refurbished and moved in with his wife and several Indian servants. The wife died a year or so later, one of the servants died in 1954, and Colonel Pemberton himself gradually deteriorated in health and mental powers, finally passing on late in 1961. The Locks took over the following year.

Mr Benbow gave me one other piece of information. Apparently the road had been constructed in the 1890s and occupied what had been the grounds of a large house known as 'The Grange', hence the name Grange Walk. Armed with this tit-bit, I went to the local library and looked up old maps of the town. These showed clearly a large area of wooded land where Grange Walk now lay, and in the middle of this area was a building marked 'The Grange'; I estimated that it had been situated roughly where No. 13 now stood.

I followed this up by calling on the local vicar. He had only been resident in the town for some ten years, but he had access to an enormous amount of information contained in old parish documents and books in his archives. After a deal of patient searching, he discovered that 'The Grange' had been pulled down in 1889, shortly after the sudden death of the then owner, Sir Geoffrey Rochemont. His demise came about as the result of falling out of a top floor window, and at the time had been deemed an accident. He had been living alone, his wife having died some three years earlier: they had had no issue.

And that was it. My researches ended there. By this time the surveyor's report had come to hand and as soon as I read it I realised I now had to make a quick decision, or the house might be snapped up by someone who appreciated its true worth.

My wife also read the report – twice – then looked at me.

"Well?"

"Well what?" I countered, to gain time. It was, I confess, on the way to becoming a habit of mine, and one that must have been irritating to other people. But Sandra refused to get annoyed.

"It's good, isn't it?" she asked, employing her usual and very feminine device of pretending to acknowledge that I knew more about technical matters than she did.

"It's excellent. In fact, it couldn't be better."

"So what's there to stop us going ahead – before the rest of the vultures get the scent?"

I drew a deep breath.

"You know that I've not been able to find anything to explain that feeling I get in the master bedroom. Oh sure – the house has seen plenty of deaths – more than its fair share, I imagine. It's even possible that many of them occurred in that same bedroom, but there's nothing to indicate that anything other than natural causes was involved. The house was once supposed to be haunted, but that often happens to houses left empty for years. In short, there's absolutely *no* reason for not going ahead with the purchase."

"But . . ." she prompted.

"No buts," I replied sharply. "I'm not going to let a vague and wholly irrational fear affect my decision. If you're happy, we'll go ahead and make our offer."

"I'm happy," she responded. "I only hope you will be."

"Time will tell."

I have to confess that I pitched my offer as low as I dared, half-hoping that the vendor would reject it out of hand, or that someone else would make a better offer. Surprise wrestled with unease when my solicitor rang back within the hour to report that Mrs Lock had accepted my bid and that he would begin work on the usual legal procedures immediately.

I remember that, after I had replaced the receiver at the end of the call, I sat quite still for a long time, feeling a knot of acute apprehension form in my stomach. I felt I was trapped, that I had been manoeuvred by vast and irresistible forces into a long dark tunnel, and that I was being remorselessly impelled towards the end, where there lay in store for me some fearful fate that I knew nothing about, yet dreaded beyond words. And, once I had conveyed the good news to Sandra, I knew that I had set the seal on my fate. She took the news much as I had expected, with pleasure because she knew as well as I did that it was the right house for us, but also with doubt because she was aware of my feelings. After giving it some thought, she made a suggestion which echoed one taking shape in my mind; we would ask Mrs Lock if we could examine the master bedroom, just in case there was any pointer to what it was that affected me so badly. This would also determine whether or not the effect was still present, or had merely been a temporary thing – perhaps due to my having been under the weather at the time.

Accordingly I took the plunge and telephoned Mrs Lock. In order to obtain her agreement and co-operation, I had to be quite frank about the reason for what was clearly an unusual request and her reaction was much as I had anticipated. She expressed great surprise and said that she had slept in that bedroom ever since they had moved into the house and she had never suffered any ill-effects, mental or physical. But she was very understanding and said that if we cared to go along that evening we could have 'carte blanche' to poke around all we wanted, without interference.

I accepted her offer and we went round at once. Any hopes I may have entertained that the animosity I had encountered at the first visit was a 'one-off' exercise died an immediate and unhappy death as I accompanied my wife up the drive. It was still there, invading my body with tendrils of fears as we waited at the front door, lapping at my mind as we traversed the hall and climbed the stairs, seizing my heart in ice-cold fingers as we entered the fateful room. Sandra glanced at me and said, "It's still there then?"

"Yes," I replied, striving to keep my voice steady. I knew I had gone pale and my hands were shaking. Mrs Lock looked at me curiously.

"You feel something?"

I nodded, fearing that if I spoke my voice would reveal my agitation.

"What sort of something? Can you describe it?"

I tried to put my fears into words, realising even as I did so that my powers of description were quite inadequate to convey the sheer horror of the malignancy that menaced me. Eventually Mrs Lock shrugged. "I can't imagine what it could be." She looked at Sandra. "Do you feel anything?"

"No. As far as I'm concerned it's a delightful room."

"I'm sorry," I said. "As my wife will confirm, I'm not usually like this. I know there's something wrong, but what it is and what the cause is leaves me baffled. But I've promised her that if we can't find anything in this room then our purchase of this house will go forward as planned."

"I'll leave you to it," she said. "You're free to peer and poke about as much as you like – cupboards, drawers, the lot. I've left my things just as they are, just in case . . . well, you know . . . "

"You're very kind," I replied hastily. "Not many women would allow total strangers to pry into their things."

"I doubt I've anything to hide," she laughed. "And – to be quite frank – I do want the purchase to go through."

She withdrew and we heard her go downstairs. We commenced the search, starting with the two large built-in cupboards. One contained linen, the other Mrs Lock's outer clothing and shoes. We explored both thoroughly, tapping the inner walls for hollow spaces and the floor for cavities. We then turned our attention to the moveable furniture and Sandra went through the drawers of the dressing-table and tallboy. We looked under the double-bed, tapped the panelled walls and tested the solid oak floor.

Finally we looked at the fireplace and sought permission to uncover it. This readily given, we moved aside the electric fire and unscrewed the hardboard from its frame. This exposed an old fireplace choked with dust, leaves, pieces of brick and other refuse. It was black and sooty and, because there was a bend further up the chimney, I could not see the sky.

We searched for over an hour before we called it a day. We had been through the room as thoroughly as was possible in the circumstances, to no avail whatsoever. Nothing had been found. It was not practicable to tear down the panelling, pull up the floor-boards or remove the ceiling. Something *might* be lurking in that room, bricked up or boarded up, but we were not going to find it.

I knew I was beaten. A deep sense of desolation and foreboding filled me as I realised I was still inside that long dark tunnel, still being forced towards my fate, my appointment with destiny. I was quiet on the way home and eventually Sandra spoke.

"What now, darling?"

"We go ahead, just as I promised. There's nothing left to do. I'd be a fool to give in to what is no more than an unfounded premonition, however strong it seems."

"Not if it's as strong as you say it is," she replied without conviction.

"It's strong enough. But I'm determined to go ahead, just the same."

"Look! It'd be silly to go ahead if you really feel that strongly about it . . . "

"It'd be a damned sight sillier not to. I'm not going to live the rest of my life branded as a coward, afraid to move into a house just because the main bedroom gives me the creeps."

"You know I wouldn't feel that way about you, whatever you did," she said.

"Maybe you would, and maybe you wouldn't. But I would. And it's me that has to live with me, if you see what I mean. So no more arguments – no more shilly-shallying. I'm going ahead."

And I did. Contracts were exchanged in four weeks, duly signed, and the ponderous mechanism of the law ground leisurely through to the conclusion. After another three weeks Mrs Lock moved out, and we took possession the following Saturday. During this waiting period my stomach bred apprehensive butterflies a-plenty, until my fear was a physical pain. I began to have restless nights, my disordered sleep disturbed by nightmares which were nothing more than variations on a theme. At the end of every one I awoke sweating and trembling, my wife sitting up beside me and trying to calm me. In time these bad nights had their effect on me during the day; I began to act in a nervous manner, to lack concentration in my job, to lose my appetite. Sandra noticed what was going on but with great self-control forbore to draw attention to it.

Somehow I carried on, both with my work and with the many problems concerning the house-purchase. The day for moving in came closer and each day I had to fight harder to control the sickening dread that now occupied my mind like a malignant growth. Towards the end my will faltered and I felt like running away, but the negotiations had by this time reached the point of no return and in any case I was given a lot of support by Sandra, who continued to bolster my flagging ego and helped to sustain me whenever I felt like ditching it. Without her encouragement I could not have carried on: with it I was able to struggle through.

Moving day, when it came, was fine and the occupation of the house took place without trouble or hindrance. My wife and I had arranged to move in first and get settled before our dependents joined us. Thus it was that, when the removal men had departed, around 5pm, we were left on our own.

Mrs Lock had left all carpets and curtains, so that, once we had installed all our furniture and effects, the house took on a different, more homely, aspect, so much so that my wife commented on it.

"What a difference one's own bits and pieces make," she said, looking round the living-room. The French windows were wide open to the sunlit garden and in fact I had already made a note that the grass needed cutting. "Mrs Lock had some nice stuff, but there's nothing like one's own things. Don't you agree?"

"Mm," I responded, trying to infuse some enthusiasm into my voice. She glanced at me sharply and the pleasure in her face died out. There was a short silence during which (I guessed) she was framing her next question.

Finally she said, "Is it as bad as ever?"

As soon as we had entered the house that morning I had been

forced to confess that the same old feelings of apprehension had attacked me. The initial impact of the empty house had almost compelled me to flee, but somehow I had fought it off and tried to obliterate it from my mind. Then when the removal men had arrived, I'd been so occupied with the resultant activity that my obsession had receded to the back of my consciousness. Even in the master bedroom I had been able to deal with the fear. But now, although there was still much to do, we were physically exhausted and resting with a cup of tea. And as a result the feeling of utter dread came surging back, so badly that I could hardly think straight. I barely heard Sandra speak, but when she repeated her question I forced myself to reply.

"It's just as bad – if not worse."

"I'm sorry."

She got up and came over to sit on the arm of my chair.

"I have to be honest. Whatever it is that affects you, it doesn't touch me. As far as I'm concerned this is a perfect house. But I can see you're feeling – well, at the very least, pretty low. And you probably feel all the worse because there's no apparent reason. But, now we've actually moved in and all the boring preliminaries are over, I honestly think you'll start to feel much better. Get today over . . . or, better still, tonight . . . and I really think you'll begin to forget this – this shadow which seems to hang over you. Don't forget I shall be here *all* the time. It isn't as though you'll have to sleep in that room all by yourself. And I promise you I won't leave your side until you're your old self again. How does that sound?"

I allowed her words to sink in, hoping they would be balm to my apprehensions, but I could not in truth say they made me feel more confident. Nevertheless I managed to raised a smile.

"Thank you, my dear. I don't know what I'd do without you. And perhaps you're right: give me a few days . . . It might be – what do they call it? – psychosomatic: I've got a slight physical disorder and it's affecting my mind."

"Possibly. The best answer is to keep busy: there's still plenty to do."

We went on working until the shadows thrown by the trees

fringing the garden lengthened across the lawn and finally merged into a huge abyss of darkness. And, as night grew, so did my fears. At ten-thirty, when we had drawn the curtains across the darkened windows and were sitting over a last hot drink, I have to admit that I was in a pretty pitiable state of nerves. I was shaking – I could not help it – and my heart was thumping like the proverbial steam-hammer. Yet nothing had happened; neither of us had experienced any unusual sights or sounds; no apparitions had appeared before us; no 'bumps-in-the-night' had been heard; no inexplicable occurrences: nothing untoward at all. I tried to convince myself it was just another house, just another construction of bricks and mortar and timber, made by ordinary people so that other ordinary people could live in it. But no amount of rationalisation made any difference. Finally my wife said, "We're both tired out. Let's have an early night. I suggest that you take a couple of your capsules. OK?"

I agreed only too readily. I was eager to consider anything to alleviate the deep dread that held me like a coffin holds its occupant. Good God, I thought desperately, I was even thinking up morbid analogies!

We went round the house making sure that the doors and windows were securely fastened. I could not refrain from peering out through the curtains at the back garden. At the rear all was black shadow, plus a deathly silence made more intense by the sighing of the wind in the trees. I could not see lights in any of the adjacent houses, but this was not surprising as the garden was surrounded by trees and thick, high bushes. At the front it was also dark and shadowy, but an occasional car passed along the road which lay the other side of the thick Leylandii hedge. Here again I could see no lights in the houses. The sound of traffic should have been reassuring, but it was not.

As we entered the main bedroom, the feeling of unutterable terror assailed me once again. I felt suffocated by what seemed like an invisible ocean of fear. I performed my ablutions in a daze, swallowed a couple of my capsules and climbed into bed. I lay rigid, shaking as though I had the ague, fighting the panic and the apprehension that continually assaulted my senses. I watched my wife prepare for bed, sitting in her green nightgown at the dressing-table as she removed her make-up. I stared round the room with bulging eyes. I had put a 150-watt bulb in the light fitment and the room was flooded with light. I could see the two double-door cupboards, full now with our clothes, and I found myself wondering what might be lurking in their recesses. I stared at the boarded-up fireplace and my mind conjured up black apparitions that might even now be waiting to break out into the room. I saw the curtains swaying in the slight movement of night air and heard the Virginia Creeper rustling in the breeze – or was there some monstrosity out there? I looked up at the ceiling and wondered what diabolical entity lived in the spaces between the ceiling and the floor above, or in the rooms overhead, or even in the cavernous loft. I thought about the floor beneath us and what might inhabit the dark and cobwebbed cavities beneath it. I visualised the dark silent garden and the unmentionable monsters that might even now be oozing their way towards the house . . .

But gradually the sleeping capsules exerted their blessed and benign influence and began to allay the trepidation that had kept me in its grip far too long. Almost imperceptibly the fear dwindled as consciousness ebbed. I was only vaguely aware of Sandra as she came over to the bed and switched on her bedside lamp.

"How are you feeling now?" she asked softly.

I answered drowsily, only too desirous of letting this heavenly lethargy take full possession of me.

"That's good," she said. "Everything's quiet: you can drift off to sleep with an easy conscience."

She climbed into bed and I was hardly conscious of her warm nightgown-clad body nudging mine. The bedside lamp was extinguished and we lay in darkness. Almost at once my new and welcome mood of insouciance dropped from me, exposing me once more to the icy fingers of dread. I stared wildly up into the blackness, realising that this was, for me, the moment of truth – the moment in time when, despite the warm human body beside me, I was well and truly *alone*. My heart began to beat faster . . . my body was suddenly wet with sweat . . . the hair at the back of my neck prickled anew. The unspeakable malevolence battered at me in hot stifling waves. Once more I fought in grim silence to remain calm, to combat this unseen and illogical invasion of my mind, and gradually the capsules reasserted their influence. I became aware that the darkness was not total: a faint glow, presumably from the street-lamp in the road, filtered through the curtains, and an inch-wide gap between the pair at the right-hand window admitted a pale ray of light that painted a yellow line down the wall above the bed. Somehow this seemed to quieten my fears and slowly but surely I drifted off again . . .

. . . to start suddenly to full wakefulness. I stared up into the dark, wondering where I was. The faint glow of light from the windows, and the thin ray of light still striking across the room, brought me to full realisation, both of my whereabouts and my recent experiences. I had no idea how long I had been asleep, but it was as quiet as the grave both in the room and outside. In fact the whole house was silent, but to my disordered mind it was not the silence of a dull suburban dwelling but of an alien life-form, alive yet not alive, waiting with infinite patience, waiting . . . for what? I lay rigid, not daring even to move my arm to look at my watch. I had no idea of the time. My heart raced and my limbs sweated as the sick dread with which I was so familiar came back, redoubled in intensity, to possess and claim my mind, body, soul, brain and indeed my whole self. The capsules, I knew, were useless: my defences were down and I was totally exposed to the unutterably loathsome malignancy that now rolled at me in waves of suffocating terror. I was alone, pinned down in my bed in that dreadful room, helplessly vulnerable to the monstrous emanations of inhuman venom beating at me, swamping me. I was paralysed with fright as my bemused mind slowly absorbed the fact that at long last it was here! Here, in this black evil room in this house of horror, the unthinkable entity that right from the start had haunted and terrified me was now stalking me, holding in its ghastly paws the dreadful fate for which I had been hideously predestined.

In an access of fear I writhed – and quite by accident touched the body of my sleeping wife. With an immense surge of relief I realised that I was, after all, not alone. Sandra, my wife, my life-partner, my sweetheart, still lay beside me, warm, soft, feminine and entirely human: even now I could turn to her for succour, for support, for sympathy and help. In the midst of my terror I found the necessary strength and will-power to turn towards her and pluck feebly at her sleeping form, saying in a hoarse voice "Sandra, my love, wake up! Please wake up and help me."

But what I touched was not warm, not soft, not feminine, not in the remotest sense human. And when it swivelled, slowly and deliberately, towards me and with awful stealth and fearful purpose rose up in the bed and towered menacingly over me, I knew that I was about to die, and die in a most ghastly way. I uttered a choked scream and my flailing hand touched, and grasped, the bedside lamp . . .

V

The King's Head

If you leave Cheltenham by one of the main roads (and I do not propose to say which one) you will see, on your left, a brand-new public house. For the purposes of this story I shall call it the 'King's Head'. It is not merely new: it is, I regret to say, aggressively new. Constructed of a garish red brick, with extensive stainless steel and a lot of plate glass, the exterior reminds one of a small factory. Inside it is decorated on the theme of a game of chess, the walls resplendent in lilac and maroon squares (chess-board pattern) and carved wooden replicas of chess-pieces inside every other square and on the ends of the oak benches. There is, alas, the ubiquitous juke-box, although I'm pleased to be able to say that the selection of disks excludes the more extreme forms of modern 'music'. Mine host, a tall bulky ex-amateur boxer named Ray Brookes, dresses most of the time in a conservative business suit and only takes his jacket off when the temperature in the bar exceeds 80 degrees. His wife, Nancy, is attractive in a somewhat blatant fashion: blonde-haired, well-rounded and cheerful, she plays her part in attracting trade by wearing tight sweaters and low-cut blouses and resting her over-developed bosom on the bar-top whilst chatting with the customers.

Like most hostelries of a similar nature, it has a large adjoining carpark, and exceedingly busy lunch-time trade – and a ghost.

You may be surprised to hear that a modern flashy roadhouse

of this description should have a ghost.

So was I.

Let me tell you about it.

I have to confess that I do not normally patronise such establishments as the King's Head, preferring the older village-inn type of place, but I was out with a colleague one day and since we were passing the pub about the time refreshments were indicated, he suggested we went inside. He had been there before, apparently, and not only knew the wife Nancy rather well but had experienced their 'Chicken in the Basket' and recommended it without reserve.

Within a few minutes we were seated at the bar, pint tankards at our elbows, our food on order, and I was being introduced to Nancy. You may judge that it was a warm day when I tell you we were quaffing iced lager and that Nancy's blouse was so décolleté that I feared for the imminent exposure of both of her best-known assets.

We were early, and her husband was dealing adequately with the other customers, so Nancy was free to talk with us. Naturally I broached the subject of the pub's modernity, and in reply she informed me that (1) it was in fact only five years old, (2) that it replaced an ancient inn that had been in existence for over three hundred years, and that (3) there was a ghost.

Immediately I pricked up my ears.

"A ghost?" I repeated. Then, rather tactlessly, I added, "This place?"

"And what exactly do you mean by 'this place'?" she challenged, her heavily made-up eyes sparkling with incipient indignation.

"Sorry!" I said hastily. I ignored my friend's chuckle. "Nothing wrong with your establishment, ma'am – nothing at all. Very smart, very comfortable, good beer, and Roger here tells me the food would make Egon Ronay drool. But – I mean – well, it *is* a bit new, isn't it? How come it has a ghost?"

"I like new pubs," replied Nancy, a touch mollified. "I can

assure you I've had it up to here with oak beams that crack your head open, crevices full of dirt and dust, cellars with nests of cockroaches in 'em, narrow stairs where you can break your leg before breakfast, etcetera, etcetera . . . "

"Yes, I grant all that. But what about this ghost?"

"Well, to tell you the truth, it isn't strictly a ghost. More your poltergeist type of thing, actually. And I suppose, when you come right down to it, it isn't really ours, anyway."

"Would you care to elaborate on that?" I asked with a grin.

"Well – we sort of inherited it – from the old inn that used to stand on this site."

Needless to say, this only made me feel more intrigued, but just then the doors opened and a crowd of lunch-time drinkers and diners flooded in and Nancy had to excuse herself. Her husband was equally busy and I resolved to return at a less busy time and try to worm the story out of anyone prepared to be so treated.

Accordingly I went back one evening, on a day which my friend assured me was the one on which I'd be most likely to receive a sympathetic hearing. He proved to be right: within five minutes I was supping ale with Ray Brookes himself in a corner of the spacious and almost-empty room. I was, as usual, being somewhat abstemious, but he was halfway through his fifth pint and just warming up. When I broached the subject of the ghost, he grinned.

"One way of dragging in the customers," he remarked. "Not as much fun as topless dancing girls, but a lot cheaper."

I experienced a wave of disappointment.

"You mean it's nothing but a gag? No ghost?"

"Oh yes, there's a ghost all right," he replied casually. "Bit of a nuisance at times. Especially as it's not exactly ours."

"Not yours?"

"What, and this place only five years old? Do me a favour! No, it belongs to the old pub that used to be here. Somehow it got transferred."

"How?"

"Don't ask me. I'm not much up on that sort of thing. Don't believe in ghoulies and ghosties and long-leggy beasties, and things that go bump in the night."

"Long-leggety, actually."

"Pardon?"

"The actual quotation refers to long-leggety beasties. But hold on! If you don't believe in them, how come you admit to having one? Not exactly consistent, is it?"

"Well, for one thing it's good for business. A lot of people come here just to say they've visited a haunted pub. I sometimes think of laying one on specially for them. The other thing . . . " He paused, then went on gamely, " . . . let's say I'm prepared to keep an open mind on the subject."

"Have *you* seen or heard anything weird?"

He looked a bit sheepish. "Well, in so many words . . . yes. I've heard it, anyway. We all have: Nancy there, and the kids."

"What have you heard?"

"A banging door."

"Come again?" I requested.

"A banging door. A door – you know – banging – in the middle of the night."

"What else?"

"Nothing else."

"Nothing at all? Has no one ever *seen* anything?"

"No, not a thing."

"So your so-called ghost is nothing other than a banging door?"

"Well, I suppose it's true to say we don't actually *know* that it's a banging door. It just sounds like one."

I was half-intrigued, half-disappointed. "You can't leave it like that," I said. "Tell me more."

"It'll cost you another pint of the same."

I fetched refills and reseated myself by him. As I did so, I said, "So you've no idea what it is or what causes it?"

"No."

"Does it happen frequently?"

"Oh God, no. Once or twice a year at the most, and then only during the night. I suppose you could say we've got used to it."

"And you've not been able to trace it?"

86

"No."

"Nor find out what it is?"

"No. Like I said, it sounds just like a door banging, not too far away. When we first began to hear it, I went over the whole place, from ground floor to roof, inch by inch. Didn't find a damn thing." He took a long swig from his tankard. "Bloody funny thing though: wherever you go in the place, you never get any nearer to it. It's there – somewhere – but you don't know where. It's not far away, but . . . "

"What about your kids?"

"They've got used to it, same as Nancy and me."

"No. What I really mean is, well . . . you don't think they might be responsible . . ?"

"No." He laughed. "I had the same idea at first – for a while – but it happened when they were away."

"Something to do with the plumbing – wiring – timbers shrinking?"

"No way. You forget, it existed long before this place was built."

"Oh yes, that's right. You said it got transferred from the old King's Head."

"Yes. Seems it was much the same then. Happened regularly, apparently, and the landlord and his wife got used to it. But he had quite a story about it. Seems that, about a hundred years ago, someone went looking for it – and found it."

"No! Tell me more."

He looked across at the bar and some kind of unspoken message passed between him and Nancy.

"OK. It's not too busy at the moment." He raised his tankard to his lips and drained it swiftly and competently. "I first heard about it from a regular from the old King's Head who started to come here when this was built, didn't like it and sheered off to the Crown. Well, he was no great loss: used to spend all evening hunched up over a single pint. But I was in conversation with him on one occasion and he told me a bit of the story, then said I could probably get the rest from the landlord of the old pub. Fellow named Joe Boddington: retired when they pulled his pub down and moved to Cirencester." Ray Brookes grimaced. "Actually, he's dead now: I read about it in the *Morning Advertiser*. Over eighty when he shuffled off to that great public house in the sky: hope I live that long."

"Anyway, I went to see Joe at Cirencester. Found him digging in his back garden – and he was nigh on eighty then! Big fellow he was, stooped with age, but even then he was no shorter than me. He had a round very red face, thick white sideburns, even thicker white moustache: reminded me of Jimmy Edwards (remember him?) except Joe was taller. Came from the west country years before and still had a lot of Devonshire cream and cider in his voice, know what I mean? He was a bit reticent when I told him why I'd come to see him, but we adjourned to his local and under the influence of a few pints he mellowed and told me the whole story.

"Well, it was a weird enough yarn and I'm hanged if I believe even half of it, but later on I managed to get some corroboration from other sources – and the builders of this place had an interesting tail-piece to it all. However, first things first."

And Ray, having ordered refills, settled back and proceeded to tell me the full story, which I now set out below in my own words.

It happened well over a hundred years ago – in the 1870s, Ray thought. There was a man and wife in charge of the old King's Head then – a couple by the name of Smith, which I suppose was a pretty common name even in those days. They were both getting on in years, but they kept a tidy house and besides the bar trade there were a number of rooms to let. The inn had been built several hundred years before and it was a huge old barn of a place by all accounts, all ancient beams, low ceilings, inglenooks, narrow spiral staircases, lots of rooms here, there, everywhere, with no apparent sense to their location, and corridors that twisted and turned and went round corners without seeming to get anywhere. I suspect there'd been a lot of additions and extensions to the original structure over the years. Apparently people would book in down at the bar, be given the key to their room, go up the narrow wooden stairs to the first floor – and appear a quarter of an hour later with a sheepish look on their face and say they'd got lost. The upper floors were known as the Rabbit Warren and it was a bit of a joke with the regulars when a newcomer disappeared upstairs with his bags and his key, and everyone would lay bets on how long it would be before he came down again.

One evening they thought they were going to have another chance of gambling with their hard-earned cash when a young couple booked in – a young man in his middle twenties and a wife two or three years younger. It soon emerged that they had not been married for very long. They were a pleasant enough pair: the man tall, dark and good-looking, the girl small and winsome. Apparently they were on their way north to visit an uncle in Harrogate and they booked in for three nights: it seems they were in no great hurry to meet up with their avuncular relative.

As they registered, under the inquisitive eyes of the regulars, more than one young roysterer in the bar must have wished he were taking the husband's place that night. The Frobishers (that was their name) were given the key to room 17 and, as they mounted the stairs, the girl preceding her husband (who carried their bags), the locals began to lay their bets. The greatest amount of money went on the man reappearing in fifteen minutes or less, although one or two of the more discerning customers placed their shillings on the chance that the couple would not be back down at all.

The latter group of punters was lucky: the Frobishers did not return that evening. According to Elisha Smith, they had supper in their room and the flickering light from their candles (visible in the wide crack beneath their door) went out at eleven-thirty.

Two hours later – about one-fifteen in the early morning – Elisha Smith and his good lady were woken up by an unusual noise. Moonlight entered their room through a gap in the curtains and they stared at one another in puzzlement. After some sleepy discussion, they decided that it was only a door banging somewhere within the inn, although this was a little surprising as there was no wind that night. Elisha rose from the bed, donned robe and slippers, took a lighted candle and set out to find, and close, the offending portal. He stood outside the bedroom door, listening, decided it came from the floor below (they slept up on the second floor) and descended the stairs to begin his search.

But he had no luck at all. In fact, he was still looking when the noise suddenly ceased. He waited a few minutes, the darkness relieved only by the flickering flame from his candle, but nothing further disturbed the silence and he went back to bed.

Next morning, as he served the Frobishers with a hearty breakfast, he enquired if they had heard a door banging during the night. Mr Frobisher said they had, and he had been on the point of getting up to do something about it when it stopped. His wife, who seemed to have quite a will of her own, added that she had been considerably incommoded by it, and hoped that it would not happen again. Elisha assured her that it was most unlikely.

Next day was a busy one for the landlord and he totally forgot the incident of the previous night. But when the last customer had staggered out into the mild and very dark night, and the inn door had been locked and bolted, and he was in the bedroom preparing for sleep, there was some discussion between him and his wife Hannah regarding the possibility of the noise being heard again. Elisha could not believe that it would happen again, especially as nothing had been heard during the day, and the night was both warm and windless. However, he admitted that he had been surprised at his inability to find the door in question, bearing in mind that he had been living in the house for many years. He pondered on the problem as he lay in bed, and soon fell asleep.

It seemed to him that he had been unconscious for only a short while when he found himself wide awake, ears pricked up.

The door was banging again.

He lay for a while, hoping it would stop. Hannah woke up as well and demanded to know what he was going to do about it. It was not so much loud as persistent and, in the absence of any satisfactory explanation, decidedly aggravating. They agreed that it definitely came from the floor below – the first floor – and Elisha was getting up when they both became aware of other sounds – the noise of a door opening, a shuffling of slippered feet, a creaky floorboard. He put on his robe and slippers, lit a candle and made his way down to the first floor.

Almost at once he was aware of the flickering light from another candle and, behind it, the tall figure of Mr Frobisher, clad in resplendent dressing-robe and felt slippers, his hair tousled and his face alert. He told Elisha that both he and his wife had been woken up by the banging door and she had been so perturbed by the noise that she had persuaded him to take immediate action. The innkeeper was full of profuse apologies and said he would make sure *this* time that the offending door was found and permanently secured. He swore that he would, if necessary, nail it up. Frobisher, who seemed a sensible sort of fellow, suggested that they search for it together, starting at one end of the floor and finishing at the other. Elisha was doubtful, as even he was not certain where the floor started or finished, but he recommended the top of the stairway down to the ground floor as a good starting-place, so they went to that spot and began their investigation.

Ten minutes later they were back where they had started, having failed to find anything. Both were puzzled and Mr Frobisher waxed somewhat sarcastic at the expense of the innkeeper in regard to his inability to deal with what seemed a simple matter. Elisha was sufficiently spirited to argue with the other and in fact extracted from him an admission that the whole thing was inexplicable. The door continued to bang, but they could not find it, nor were they able to reach any point where it became any louder or clearer. After a brief discussion it was agreed that they could do no more and they both returned to their respective beds.

The visitor entered his room to find his wife in a state of the most extreme agitation. It seemed that the persistent and monotonous banging of the door, which seemed to her to be quite near and therefore easy to find, had at first disturbed her repose and then played acutely on her nerves, so that her husband found her pale-faced, trembling and not far from collapse. He spent some time attempting to allay her fears and eventually persuaded her to go back to bed on the understanding that he would tackle the innkeeper about their leaving the King's Head a day earlier than planned.

The following morning found them talking to Elisha Smith as he served their breakfast (not that Mrs Frobisher was in a state to eat anything). She was as anxious to leave as she had been the previous night, but her husband had been having second thoughts and he was now reluctant to do anything precipitate: firstly because it was impossible for them to arrive at his uncle's any earlier than planned, and no other bookings had been made: and secondly because the weather had taken a turn for the worse. Rain was now falling on the inn and the surrounding countryside and showed no signs of abating: as a consequence, despite his wife's desire to leave, he was far from keen on venturing forth. The young visitors, who when they first arrived had appeared to be a real pair of turtle-doves, now engaged in a low-voiced but distinctly acrimonious argument over the breakfast-table and Elisha had to step in to attempt to heal what was beginning to look like a sizeable breach. They appeared to be glad of his opinion and the three of them talked at length. When Elisha told them he was bringing in a number of qualified men from the nearby town to check the inn inch by inch, and that very day, Mr Frobisher made the decision to stay and his unhappy wife had no option but to accept the verdict.

Elisha took the wagon and pair to the town that same morning and returned in time for lunch with a team of builder's men, led by a capable-looking man named Partridge. They brought with them a formidable battery of tools and, after a hearty lunch, proceeded to scatter about the old hostelry and go over it with a fine toothcomb. Apart from Partridge, there were ten of them and they spent seven hours on the job. At the end of that time many doors had been adjusted, but no cause for the noise had been found. Partridge, although saying very little, showed by his manner what he thought of a man who had called him out on a fool's errand, and most of his men agreed with him, but one oldster – in his seventies but still hale and hearty – dissented.

"Oi believe um," he said, nodding his white head. "It be a-calling from beyond the grave, mark my words. It baint of this world, that be for sartin. Take moi 'eed, su'thin' mortally wrong be a-foot 'ere." And when asked, by one jocular companion, what he thought ought to be done, he replied, "Knock it down and foind what be amiss."

But his views were derided and Partridge took his team away, although not before collecting the agreed fee from a disappointed innkeeper.

It was unfortunate that Mrs Frobisher had chanced to overhear the old man's gloomy prognostications and was not reassured by them. But her husband – and Elisha – spent some time explaining the long and comprehensive survey that had that day been carried out, and that it was ninety-nine per cent certain there would be no repetition. She remained unconvinced, well aware that the remaining one per cent could be significant.

Thus it was that she went up to bed that night in a very discomposed state of nerves. In those days there were no tablets to help, nor was there any laudanum available, nor any doctor living nearby, and her husband was quite unable to calm her. It is therefore not surprising that, when the door started banging in the middle of the night, she woke at once and was immediately in such a state of nerves that her husband, although despairing of any success, got up and went out into the dark, bearing a candle. On his way round he encountered Elisha and they conducted yet another search, whilst the banging continued.

And yet again the same result was achieved – nothing.

Returning to the bedroom, Mr Frobisher had to admit to his now frantic wife that he had been unsuccessful. But this time she refused to accept his statement.

"I can hear it quite distinctly," she said in a quivering voice. "It must be near this room. If you cannot find it, I will. Hand me the candle."

"If you insist," he said reluctantly, realising that in her present frame of mind she would not be gainsaid. "But I will accompany you."

"No," she said with intense feeling. "You will fluster me. I will go on my own."

Mr Frobisher was thunderstruck at the amazing vehemence in

her words and, fearing opposition would make things worse, he handed over the candle.

"You men!" she said shrilly. "You can never find anything. It can only be but a step or two from here."

She went out into the dark passage and her husband watched the flickering glow from the candle-flame die away down the corridor. He was somewhat perturbed by hearing her talk to herself.

"It cannot be far away," she muttered. "I can hear it most clearly. It is along this way, without a doubt. Men!"

There followed a short silence, during which Mr Frobisher decided to go after his wife. He spent a short while finding and lighting another candle, then went outside into the passage. But the glow from his wife's candle was no longer visible. He was about to call out to her – discreetly – when he heard her talking to herself again. This time her voice was faint, as though further away.

"It is here somewhere. I can hear it quite distinctly. Round this corner . . . along this passage . . . " A pause. "Why, *there* it is!" Her voice expressed both surprise and relief. "Quite plain to see. Oh my goodness, those men!"

Mr Frobisher was unaccountably struck by a sudden access of unreasoning fear. He cried out her name and went along the passage, but as he did so his straining ears caught the unmistakable sound of a door closing. It was a sound (as he said afterwards) of such finality that he cried out "Mary!" and ran desperately along the corridor, shielding the guttering flame of his candle with his trembling hand. He stopped suddenly, as another hideous sound reached his ears – the dreadful sound of a locked door being rattled. He turned the bend in the corridor, but the light from his candle illuminated only the oak floor, the panelled walls, the low ceiling. Of his wife there was no sign. He ran to the next bend, turned it and held his candle aloft.

Nothing.

Once more the unseen door rattled, this time in a more agitated fashion, and now he heard his wife's voice, muffled and uneasy.

"It will not open. It must be locked. Henry! I have found the door, but it has become fastened and I cannot get out. Please help me."

Henry Frobisher felt the icy finger-tips of inexplicable horror.

"Mary!" he shouted. "Don't worry. I'm coming. Where are you? I can hear you but cannot see you. Talk to me so that I know where you are."

But the only answer he got was another rattle at the door. Then his wife spoke again, and her voice was shrill and alarmed.

"Help! I am locked in. Henry! Mr Smith! Please help me. I cannot get out."

Mr Frobisher forced himself to remain calm. "Mary, I can hear you. You are not far away. Please tell me which room you are in and I will come and let you out."

But all he got for his pains was a frenzied rattle of a doorknob and his wife crying, in a pitiful voice, "Help! Henry, where are you? I am locked in. Please will someone come and let me out."

Henry's heart almost stopped as he realised that, although he could hear her, she could not hear him. This he could not understand, but he forced himself to control his anxiety and proceeded to search the corridor and every room off it, meanwhile repeatedly calling her name. It did not make his task any easier to hear, every now and again, a frantic rattle of a door-handle, and cries for help that grew more and more hoarse and panic-stricken.

Elisha Smith arrived on the scene, having been roused by the shouts and cries. He was truly shaken by Mr Frobisher's story, and became even more perplexed when he himself heard Mrs Frobisher's voice, tearfully pleading, almost incoherent by now, interspersed by spasmodic rattling. Willingly he joined his guest in the search, only to admit at the end to total bafflement.

No trace of Mrs Frobisher could be found

Elisha went to his neighbours, roused them, and they searched the entire building, still without result. Mr Frobisher wandered aimlessly about, hither and thither, now well-nigh demented by the mental agony of continually hearing his wife's voice. Sometimes she cried out, her voice laden with terror: sometimes she pleaded, sobbing bitterly: sometimes she sounded hysterical, screaming and moaning, laughing and crying in turn: occasionally there was nothing but silence.

The next day Elisha called in building workers from the nearby town and they made yet another search, followed by a survey, going over the inn from top to bottom, from front door to back door. No secret room was found, no hidden door, no trapped woman. Yet all were able to hear her, despite the fact that her voice was now undeniably weaker, hoarse, incoherent, her pleadings interspersed by shrieking and wailing. There were no more rattles at the door-handle. Later, when they heard her talking as though to herself, in a completely alien manner, uttering sentences of total nonsense, babbling and laughing crazily, her husband lost his reason, went berserk with mental stress and had to be restrained and, still later, removed to the nearest lunatic asylum.

It was not long before the unhappy woman ceased to make any kind of sound, and from then on there was nothing but silence.

There is little more to relate. Henry Frobisher lingered on in the asylum for several months and then committed suicide. Elisha Smith and his wife would have liked to leave the King's Head, but were obliged to stay on, because it was their only means of livelihood and after what had happened there it was virtually unsaleable.

The original cause of the trouble – the banging door – started up again years later and carried on intermittently. Elisha and Hannah learned to live with it, but needless to say they never went looking for it, nor did Joe Boddington and his wife, who took the inn over when Elisha died.

When Ray had finished his account, I sat and stared at him.

"What an extraordinary story," I commented. "Do you believe any of it?"

He shrugged broad shoulders. "We've heard the banging, remember?"

"And never been able to trace it?"

"As I told you, the first couple of times it happened we did make a thorough search. Fortunately we never found it. And when we finally got to hear the tale I've just told you, we stopped looking, thank God!"

I thought about it some more and several questions came to mind, but before I could voice them Ray got to his feet.

"Looks like trade's on the up: I'd better join Nancy." As he collected up the pots, he added, "One last thing. When they pulled the old inn down, they discovered a set of bones in the rubble. They were found to be those of a female, early twenties, reckoned to have been there since about the time Mary Frobisher disappeared." He raised his eyebrows at me. "A bit rummy that, eh?"

e

VI

Waterhatch Common

Not many miles to the east of Cheltenham lies Waterhatch Common. It is, as its name implies, a stretch of green-belt common land on the southern slopes of Cleeve Hill. It is not extensive, yet contains within its boundaries some extremely pleasant areas for picnicking, walking, horse-riding, kite-flying and all those other recreational activities pursued by the modern Englishman (and woman). There is agricultural land on three sides, and plenty of rich green grass on which to gambol, interspersed by clumps of gorse and plantations of fern: the trees stand either alone or in small groups, and are all deciduous.

Situated to the north of centre, towards the slope of the hill to the north, will be found a large monolith or standing stone, known as St. Agatha's Tump. It towers some ten feet in the air, is buried to at least half that measurement, and is three feet in diameter at the visible base. It is carved from limestone, believed by some to have been hewn in a quarry somewhere in the Cotswolds. It is thought, as far as age is concerned, to be contemporary with Stonehenge, and many people suspect that it had a similar purpose, although of course there is controversy as to what that purpose might have been. Others feel it is tied in with the old pagan religions, possibly the centre and indeed focus of barbaric rituals, perhaps the scene of ancient worship. But worship of who – or what?

There is not a lot else to say about Waterhatch Common, or

about St. Agatha's Tump, except to reveal that both feature in my next story, albeit in a subsidiary role. The story itself is interesting, if somewhat fanciful. Like many a country tale, it stretches the comprehension and defies analysis. I set it down as heard: it is for you to believe it or not, as you choose.

One evening I was in my study, at home in Leckhampton (near Cheltenham), when I was interrupted by a ring at the door. On answering it, I found on the doorstep a man aged between 35 and 40, quietly dressed, clean-shaven. Brown eyes surveyed me through spectacles with thick dark rims. He mentioned my name questioningly and, when I had answered in the affirmative, he was about to continue, but hesitated, seemingly not sure whether to speak or not.

"What exactly can I do for you?" I asked, slightly impatient to get back to my work and beginning to wonder if he was a Mormon missionary, or a member of some other equally esoteric religion, seeking a convert. Not wishing to be converted in any manner whatsoever, I was prepared to be short with him.

"I would appreciate the chance of a – a talk – with – with you."

"What about?"

"Ah!" he said, a trifle unhappily. "Well – er – it's a bit difficult to know where to – begin, actually."

"Why not at the beginning?" I suggested helpfully.

"That would, I agree, be sensible: but it is not always possible to decide where that might be. Er – would I be correct in thinking that you are interested in strange stories connected with this region of the country?"

"Yes indeed." I looked at him with renewed interest. "If you have anything to tell me in that line, then you're very welcome. Have you?"

"Yes. Well – that is – I have something of that sort. It's hardly a story though: more a set of discoveries that have been made and which, if put together in a certain way, could lead to any number of intriguing speculations."

"And if put together in some other way?"

"Could be quite meaningless. What I mean to say is: there may not be any connection at all."

"I see. Well, no I don't. But I might if you were to tell me about it. Why not come in for a coffee and a chat and you can unburden yourself. I can see you're very anxious to do so."

He agreed at once and followed me upstairs and into my living-room, where I pushed the cat off its favourite chair and motioned to my visitor to sit whilst I prepared coffee. Whilst doing so I ascertained that his name was Paul Warley and that he preferred coffee to liquor. I had no hesitation in admitting him to my home: his manner was courteous, his voice educated, his attire restrained: and his bearing and manner made a favourable impression on me.

"Do you live around here?" I called from the kitchen.

"No. My home is in St. Albans, in Hertfordshire, near London."

"I know it quite well. May I ask what you do for a living?"

"I work at the Explorers' Club in Pall Mall, London – assistant to the General Secretary."

"That must be interesting work."

"It is. But never more so than in the last month or two."

"Why?" I asked, carrying the cups of coffee into the living-room. I handed him his cup. "What happened?"

He sipped his coffee and nodded his thanks. "That's where my story starts, I suppose." I sat opposite him and looked interested. He went on, "A solicitor came to see us. I won't burden you with his name, but he was acting on behalf of his client, a Mr Geoffrey Parkes, of Aylesbury, in Bucks, who had recently come into a considerable inheritance from his aunt, Mrs Prudence Purdom, of Bournemouth. Having no offspring, she had – apart from a number of minor bequests to charities – left the bulk of her estate to him. Setting aside the monies and properties he had received, there were also a number of trunks and suitcases full of old papers, diaries, photo albums, ancient magazines – you probably know the kind of stuff old people leave behind them when they die."

I nodded. My own father had died not too far back and he had left mountains of old documents and files going back fifty years

100

or more.

"Mr Parkes started to go through them," continued Warley. "At first he was not very enthusiastic: nothing seemed to be of any value or interest. The papers were dry-as-dust documents concerned with minor legal transactions over the past forty years or so. The diaries were mostly by the old lady, each one crammed with the most amazing amount of trivia and minutiae, all in tiny almost illegible handwriting.

"He had practically decided to throw the rest away without looking at it when he found, in a corner of one of the trunks, a bundle of notebooks tied with rotting cord. He disinterred the bundle and snapped the cord. Examining the notebooks, he found them to be in good condition and in handwriting a good deal clearer that that of Mrs Purdom. They were in fact in a firm masculine hand, and surprisingly legible. If they had not been, I would not be sitting here, of course! He set them aside and later began to read them. It did not take him long to discover that they were the diaries of Mrs Purdom's father."

Warley paused and drank some more of his coffee. I remained silent and alert – I have always been a good listener.

"They were the diaries of Thomas Alexander Purdom, a man who had spent much of his short life in India, first in the army and afterwards as an explorer and traveller. Mr Parkes decided it would be best if he presented the notebooks en bloc to the Explorers' Club, as he felt this would be a more suitable home for them. Naturally, they were received with gratitude, and the task of going through them, in order to evaluate the contents – for insurance purposes and in case there was anything worth publishing – fell to me. I was, of course, delighted to have both the opportunity and the responsibility, and set about my task with the keenest enthusiasm – also, I may say, with a deal of industry. I not only pursued my task during office hours, but took the notebooks home to study them in the evenings: a circumstance which I hope you will keep to yourself, as it is strictly forbidden to remove bequests from the Pall Mall offices.

"It was fascinating to read Purdom's writings, which in the main covered his life in the Indian Army and his many expeditions into the heart of what is now India and Pakistan.

"Thomas Alexander Purdom was a subaltern in the 9th Bengal Cavalry, stationed at times in Delhi, at times in Karachi, and at other times in various stations around the continent. Whilst in India he became deeply interested in Buddhism and, since army officers in those days had plenty of leave, he spent much of his time in expeditions of exploration. One of his dreams was to discover the hidden treasures of the ancient Kandyan Kings, but he was never successful. However, he became a member of the Royal Geographic Society, and was well-regarded in his time. Since his death he has sunk into obscurity and today I doubt if there is anyone who has heard of him. Sic transit gloria mundae – fame is such an ephemeral quality."

I nodded sympathetically but did not speak.

Warley continued. "When I had finished Purdom's notebooks, I realised that one particular episode in his travels remained in my mind long after the others had faded. It began in 1878 and ended, as far as he was concerned, three years later. It is this episode that forms part of my story, and the reason I came to see you."

He drained his cup, replaced it on the small table and sat back in his chair.

"Please go on – I'm all ears," I assured him, partly as encouragement and partly to fill the silence that followed his last remark.

He looked at me quizzically. "What do you know about wild children?"

I was at first startled, then rallied gamely.

"There are a few living round here who need taming," I said grimly, recalling occasions when my work had been disturbed by the excessive noise of neighbours' kids misbehaving badly.

He laughed.

"It's a term applied to those unfortunate children who are discovered in the wilds, with no known parents or family, and who have been reared by animals to such an extent that they have taken on the ways of such beasts. You may think that instances of this happening are rare, and you will therefore be very surprised to learn that over thirty such occurrences have been documented and that there must be many more that are never found and thus never known.

"When they are found, it is usually in the lair of some wild animals that have reared them as their own cubs – mostly wolves, but other animals such as leopards, bears and even pigs and sheep have been involved. The children are invariably naked, able to walk only on all-fours, have no control over their bodily functions, eat only raw food, and are either completely dumb or able to communicate only in animal-like noises. In the past attempts have been made to civilise them, but in the vast majority of cases such attempts are futile. The children, when found, have varied in age between 2 and 23, and very few have survived civilisation for more than a few years."

"Interesting," I commented. "And presumably our friend Purdom found one?"

"You catch on quickly," he replied with a smile. "Except that it was not one he found, but two."

"Do they usually come in twos?" I asked, a trifle facetiously.

He shook his head. "It is most rare."

"I'm keen to hear more," I said veraciously.

"Early in 1878 Purdom and two companions set out on an expedition into the wild and little-known country to the south-west of Delhi. The area into which they ventured was mountainous, thickly forested, and sparsely occupied by tiny settlements where the scanty indigenous population eked out a precarious existence in farming pursuits.

"I will not bore you with the details of his journey, which was hazardous but not especially eventful. But in September of that year he was encamped in a clearing near a small village called Pataguala, obliged to remain there for several days because one of his companions had come down with malaria. Purdom and his other companion – a man named Burke – spent much of their time talking with the villagers, and soon they heard about two 'manush-Bhagas' that plagued the neighbourhood. This was a native term applied to extremely hostile and fierce spirits of the forest that were part of the folklore of the region. Apparently two at least had been sighted and were described to the two

Englishmen as small apparitions, neither animal nor human, with fiery red eyes: these apparitions darted about in the jungle making queer noises resembling a cross between a snarl and a scream. They were alleged to haunt the ruins of an ancient temple which lay deep in the jungle several miles from the village.

"Purdom and Burke collected together a group of tribesmen and, guided by the headman, set off for the ruined temple. Purdom confessed to being totally confounded by the sight that greeted him and his companion when the party reached their destination – principally because the holy place bore little resemblance to the many hundreds of temples that he had seen on his journeys about the continent.

"In a clearing there were thirteen huge monoliths situated amongst rocks, bushes and dense undergrowth. Most were still standing, although a few leaned over at dangerous angles: a few lay flat and were partially obscured by thick foliage and bushes. It was not possible to see if their positioning showed any design or pattern. Many of the stone columns were carved into crude representations of bizarre creatures, some almost human, others totally bestial: these latter did not, as far as Purdom could decide, relate to any known living creature. Strange horned heads: fierce eyes in sets of two, three, four or five: scaly reptilian bodies: alien limbs: deformed appendages: and hideously-detailed modelling on the stone surface that gave a disturbing impression of hair and fur: all these confronted Purdom and Burke as they wandered with growing excitement around the steaming-hot deathly-silent jungle clearing. A few of the enormous menhirs (some were twenty feet high, others smaller) were not sculptured but bore inexplicable patterns and figures of unknown geometry, with indecipherable signs and symbols which could have been some kind of extra-terrestrial alphabet. The stones themselves must have weighed anything between 50 and 250 tons each, and Purdom could not begin to guess where they had been quarried, or how they had been transported to this lonely site in the primaeval jungle.

"But they had little time to wonder at the mysteries facing them. Some of the tribesmen, encouraged by the presence of the white men and their rifles, began to beat through the dense undergrowth and bushes around the monoliths, and in a very short while flushed out a female leopard, which leapt from a concealed hiding-place and stood glaring at them, teeth bared, its tail thrashing from side to side. Both the men were reluctant to shoot the magnificent beast, but unfortunately one of the tribesmen let loose a spear which pierced deep into the animal's shoulder. The leopard gave a terrible roar and leapt at the humans attacking her, thus forcing Purdom to shoot her to prevent loss of human life. But they had no time for regrets: the next moment the tribesmen shouted and scattered as a second leopard ran out among them. This one was younger, male, and clearly terrified of the attackers: it raced between them and fled into the surrounding jungle. Purdom and Burke let it go.

"Holding their rifles levelled and ready, the natives watching with goggling eyes, the two Englishmen approached several monoliths which lay on their sides, almost hidden by thick undergrowth. They penetrated the bush and discovered a rocky outcrop, in which was a cave. Inside the cave they found three leopard cubs and two children huddled together in a tight bunch. All five fiercely resisted attempts to part them, and eventually tribesmen had to carry the ball of struggling spitting offspring back into the clearing, where the cubs were finally disentangled from the children – who incidentally spat and hissed as much as the cubs.

"The children were a boy and a girl, the latter aged around seven, the boy a year or so younger. Both were naked, with pale skin and matted hair, and were unable to stand upright. After Purdom and Burke had recovered from their amazement at such a discovery, they quitted the area of the standing stones and took the children back with them to the village. A few days later, when the third member of the expedition was well enough to travel, they journeyed to the nearest town – Kolyagarh – where they handed the children over to Dr Khan at the small hospital there.

"The men stayed in the town for a while and had many discussions with Dr Khan. It soon became evident that neither of the two children could talk and in fact made noises similar to the leopard cubs. They ate with their mouths, crouched on all-fours, and would only eat raw meat. At first they were completely savage, fighting with the hospital staff and inflicting severe bites and scratches on many of their handlers. But the three men could not stay for ever and, after they had extracted promises that everything possible would be done for the children, they took their leave of the region."

Warley paused and took time out to clear his throat and blow his nose, both procedures accompanied by a disproportionate amount of noise.

"Incidentally," he went on after this performance. "I forgot to mention that the origin of the two children remained a mystery. Their features were anglo-saxon, their physiognomy difficult to pinpoint. Extensive enquiries were made in the towns and villages of the region, particularly among the white population, but there were no reports of any missing children over the past ten years. Even the theory that they were white was queried, some being of the opinion that they might possibly have been albino. But this matter remained, as so many others, unresolved.

"Anyway, on with my story. Six months later Thomas Alexander Purdom returned to Kolyagarh, this time on his own, in order to see how the two children had progressed in his absence. He was met by a sorrowful Dr Khan who told him that the boy – the younger of the two – had died some two months before. The efforts that had been made to rehabilitate him had been unsuccessful: he had stubbornly refused to accept the ways of the world of humans into which he had been dragged willy-nilly, and after four months of unremitting hostility aimed at the hospital staff he had managed to escape and find his way back to the circle of monoliths and to the cave where he had presumably spent all of his young life. Unfortunately the young male leopard had returned, and the cubs had grown in stature and ferocity, and the boy, instead of being welcomed back to the cave, was attacked and killed. A search party found his remains outside the cave: after the leopards and the vultures had finished their grisly work, very little was left of the poor child.

"However, on the credit side Dr Khan was able to report that the girl had so far survived and was in fact showing that she might in the fullness of time transfer her allegiance from the animal kingdom to the human race. Already patient work on the part of the hospital staff was producing results: she was losing her initial ferocity and her instinctive hatred of people, and was showing interest in food other than that to which she had become accustomed.

"Satisfied that all was being done that was possible, Purdom once again went on his way. But before he was able to revisit the hospital, he was called to active service and was sent away from India to several other parts of the British Empire, to assist in the maintenance of law and order. It was some three years before he was able to return to his old stamping-grounds and, as soon as he was in a position to take some well-earned leave, he hastened to the hospital at Kolyagarh to see how his one remaining protégé was progressing. Remembering the sad news that had greeted him on his last visit, he was somewhat apprehensive, and his fears were confirmed when he reached his destination. But this time he was not too late. Dr Patel (Dr Khan had retired a year before) told him that the girl, whom they had named Shalima, was dying, although she was still conscious and able to recognise people. Purdom went to the girl's bedside and was shocked at the thin, frail little body that lay tossing in fever under the ubiquitous mosquito-net. He requested details, but there was little to tell. Progress had been made in her reclamation: she had learned to stand upright and to eat cooked food with her hands. She had learned to control her evacuations and even to speak a few words of English. But, as in almost every other recorded instance of a similar nature all over the world, the effort needed to change from savage animal to civilised human had taken its toll. Dr Patel told Purdom that her sojourn in a gentler environment had lowered her resistance to infection and she had contracted enteric fever. He was deeply sorry to have to report that in his opinion she was very near her end.

"Despite the fact that Purdom had been away so long, he had never ceased to remember her and now her imminent death distressed him beyond words, particularly as mixed with his sadness was a great sense of guilt at leaving her in what he termed 'the lurch'. He made plans to remain in Kolyagarh indefinitely and spent long hours at the girl's bedside as she tossed and turned in delirium, applying cold cloths to her face and talking to her in a soft voice.

"The few words she had learned whilst at the hospital were basic ones such as 'food', 'drink', 'hello', 'good', 'bad', and other terms connected with her toilet. But as she lay shivering and whimpering, her lips moved frequently as though she were trying hard to say something, yet no sound emerged from her lips. She showed no signs that she comprehended anything Purdom said to her, whether in English or the local dialect, but his presence at her bedside and the soothing sound of his voice seemed to offer her some comfort, and this made his long and fatiguing vigil worthwhile. At times she lapsed into a coma very like death itself and it was at these times that Purdom feared the worst.

"Eventually, one morning about 10.15, five days after his arrival at the hospital, she fell into deep unconsciousness and Dr Patel, hastily summoned by Purdom, announced gravely that her demise was probably not more than an hour or so away.

"At 10.50 the girl appeared to regain consciousness. She gave a great shudder and her eyes slowly opened, to rest on Purdom's anxious face as he leaned over her. She was not able to see the doctor, who was standing back by the window, over which a blind had been drawn to keep out the harsh heat and light of the sun: thus he was an unseen witness to what happened next. Purdom mopped her brow once more and her eyes followed his every movement. He spoke to her softly, in English, and her eyes followed the movements of his lips.

"After a while her lips moved. He bent closer to hear her, but he had no need to do so because she spoke, suddenly and with incredible clarity, one word. Purdom turned and looked at Dr Patel, baffled."

Again Warley paused and I took the opportunity to offer a second cup of coffee, as I felt his throat might be dry after all the talking. But he refused and carried on with his account.

"According to Purdom, the word the child had spoken was 'djinn' – and Dr Patel agreed with him. But this only served to bewilder them both. Why should the girl speak of such an entity, and how had she learned about it? They knew that in India a djinn was an evil spirit – a demon of ancient Mohammedan legend supposed to have the ability to assume either human or animal form.

"But what could this girl know of such things? Purdom leaned towards her and in a gentle voice requested clarification. She may not have understood his words but she recognised his meaning. She raised her clouded eyes to his face and again said a single word 'Godman'.

"Purdom experienced once more an overwhelming sensation of sadness and regret. He told her he was no man of God, but wished he were, that he might help her. But he added that he was her friend and she could trust him. She tried to speak again, and her tongue came out to lick dry lips. Dr Patel came forward and tilted water down her throat. She swallowed and, slightly revived, said again the two words she had uttered before. The two men leaned forward to catch anything she might say, but all they heard was a final deep sigh as the last breath escaped from her lungs. The next moment her eyes closed and she died."

Warley stopped speaking. I started to say something, choked on a dry throat and coughed. Blinking, I felt my eyes were wet. Embarrassed by this unusual show of emotion, I said, "Very sad."

My visitor nodded.

"What happened after that?" I asked.

He shrugged his shoulders. "That was virtually the end of Purdom's story. He lingered on in Kolyagarh until the girl was buried, then he departed from that place and, as far as I can trace, never returned to it. His diaries went on for a few more years, in fact until his death in 1896, but there was no more mention of the wild children of Pataguala."

"However, I assume that this is not the end of *your* story?"

"No," he replied. "But you might say it's the end of the part that makes any sense. From now on, I'm afraid, it descends into perilous depths, where all is supposition, conjecture, perhaps co-incidence, almost certainly fantasy."

"Carry on," I told him. "I'm a great one for fantasy."

"Well, now I've come this far . . . "

"Exactly. More coffee?"

When I had replenished both our cups, he continued. "I do not wish to speak ill of the dead, but from his diaries one may deduce that Thomas Alexander Purdom was a serious, almost pompous man, with an undue sense of his own importance and, unfortunately, an inability to extract the essence from a mass of trivia. The accounts of his many journeys – and indeed of his life – were extremely long-winded, crammed with inessential facts and figures, and full of unnecessary self-justification and self-praise. The discovery of the wild children was in point of fact the highlight of his career and also the one episode which showed him any credit, although strangely enough he did not regard it in that light himself.

"However, it *was* this episode which stuck in my mind and the one that I discussed in detail with colleagues at the office. One of them, George Parkinson, lodges in London but is actually a Gloucestershire man, with a home and family in Prestbury, near Cheltenham."

"Ah! Do I perceive a link at last?"

"Yes indeed. I discussed with him and my other colleagues the words spoken by the girl Shalima to Purdom on her death-bed. Parkinson was at once struck by the strangeness of these words and asked to read the exact passage from Purdom's diary. He would not say why, but I noted a light in his eyes and a kind of subdued excitement that hinted at bizarre developments.

"Three days later he came into the office and without speaking handed me a piece of paper. It was a photocopy of a paragraph in a newspaper, the *Evening Telegraph* (shortly to become the *Gloucestershire Echo)*, and the date was written above the item – 13th July 1875. He told me that he had not been allowed to remove the actual newspaper from the files, nor deface the publication by cutting the paragraph out, so he had been obliged to resort to having the relevant piece photocopied. And here it is."

Warley produced a piece of paper and handed it to me. The title and date were as he had described them. The paragraph itself was in such small print that I had to use a magnifying glass to read it. It ran as follows:

110

MYSTERY DISAPPEARANCE OF
LOCAL FARMER'S CHILDREN

Farmer Silas Godman and his wife Martha, who live at Bramble Cottage just beyond the Cheltenham boundary, are distraught at the mysterious disappearance of their two children five days ago. The family had visited Waterhatch Common for recreational purposes and, whilst Farmer Godman unharnessed his mare for grazing, and Mrs Godman prepared the victuals, their daughter Jean aged 4 had taken her brother John, aged 3, across the meadow to gather buttercups. Their mother kept watch and ward on her offspring and noticed that they were playing near St. Agatha's Tump, a huge and ancient stone that has stood on the common for centuries. She states that she only removed her eyes for a moment to discourage some insects that were plaguing her and, when she looked again, the children were no longer visible, whereupon she set forth across the common to find them. When she reached the Tumulus, there was no sign of them, nor could she see them anywhere. She began to search and call about the common, and her husband came to her aid. It was he who discovered the children's clothing, two small piles of juvenile garments lying in a small hollow very near the standing stone; it was as though the children had evaporated into thin air. The distressed parents continued their search but in vain. The authorities were alerted and, although every endeavour has been made to locate the children, no trace has yet been found, nor any evidence to indicate what happened to them. The fear is that they may have been kidnapped, although it cannot be understood why their clothing was removed. One explanation is that the kidnapper was mentally deranged, but there has been no news of any such person in the vicinity. One circumstance that puzzles the authorities is that both Farmer Godman and his wife have sworn on oath that at no time did they observe any other person either at St. Agatha's Tump or on the Common, nor were the police able to find evidence of any wheeled vehicle having been nearby. Investigations are continuing.

When I had read, and reread, the item, I looked up, to encounter Warley's quizzical gaze.

"Interesting?" he asked.

"Extremely so. Was there any follow-up to this?"

"Yes. Parkinson and I went to the local newspaper offices and were permitted to go through the back files. In an issue dated 15th August of the same year there was a brief paragraph stating that up to that time extensive enquiries had produced no further news or information. Mrs Godman was in decline as a result of the terrible occurrence and the farm was going downhill.

"Two months later a further brief paragraph appeared, announcing a double tragedy. Mrs Goodman had died of a broken heart and her husband had shot himself. After that, nothing – nothing at all. We can only presume that the children were never found and the mystery never solved."

"Until now, I take it?" I said.

Paul Warley smiled.

"No doubt you'll have noticed several striking features that link the two occurrences I've detailed. Jean, aged 4 and John, aged 3, vanish on the 8th July 1875. The wild children of Pataguala were found some three years later and on examination at the hospital at Kolyagarh were thought to be 7 and 6 respectively. On the brink of death, the girl came out with two words that no one realised – why should they? – might have been her name – Jean Godman. Would it not be natural that, at the point of death, the child might have tried to convey to her listeners her own name? Surely you'll agree that the coincidence is marked."

"How was it that your friend Parkinson happened to recall the disappearance of the two children so long ago?"

"Because that very incident was resurrected in a book of short stories of Gloucestershire origin written by a Winchcombe woman and published by Matthews. It had a fair sale locally. Parkinson had it given to him as a birthday present."

"H'm. I suppose that sounds possible. But . . . ." I paused in thought. Then I said, a trifle testily, "But it doesn't make any sense. How exactly do you propose that the two children were transported from England to India in 1875? Magic carpet? And, in any case, why? Why, for God's sake?"

"I can't answer your second question – at least, not satisfactorily – but I believe I can offer a possible solution to the first," he said smugly. He paused and looked at me speculatively. "Ever heard of ley-lines?"

"Vaguely, but I've no idea what they are."

"Fellow named Alfred Watkins brought them to the public notice way back in the 1920s, in a book called *The Old Straight Track*. He had a theory that all over the British Isles there was a system of lines of energy that joined ancient sites in a pattern vaguely reminiscent of veins in a leaf, except that these lines crossed one another quite indiscriminately.

"Of course, he was not the first to suggest such a bizarre idea. The concept of a vast network of force-lines linking the remnants of ancient civilisations had been mooted before, but no *reason* or *purpose* for these were given. And naturally enough the Establishment didn't take too kindly to this new and radical idea. However, they were obliged to take note of it when, in the early 1900s, Sir Norman Lockyer, Director of the Solar Physics Laboratory, published a book which attempted to prove that, just as the Egyptian pyramids were thought to be linked with the sun, so most of the ancient sites and monuments in the UK were similarly solar-oriented, and interconnected in some mysterious and inexplicable fashion.

"His ideas were naturally ridiculed because of lack of plausibility, but since then other eminent scholars have jumped on the bandwagon and tried to show that most of the old religious structures, such as megaliths, temples, pyramids, etc., were planned and constructed with a high degree of expertise and science. Admiral Boyle Somerville was one: another was Dr Alexander Thom."

Warley broke off to make a wry grimace.

"Sorry! This has become something of an obsession with me in the last few weeks. I have found that similar studies have been carried out on the fantastic patterns in the deserts of South Peru, near Nazca, whilst even the Russians have theorised that the whole of the globe is covered by an invisible grid of force-lines.

Their idea is that the world was formed as a huge crystal and, whilst time has moulded it into the shape it is today (and what a sad shape that is!) there remains still the skeleton of the original crystalline structure, at least on the surface, linking important locations and thus providing paths for unknown forces.

"All of this merely shows that Watkins wasn't the first with the concept, but it was *his* book that brought it out into the open. As always, it met with a great deal of opposition. Some of his opponents were quick to point out that there were so many ancient monuments scattered about the UK that, statistically, some just *had* to line up. Another objection was that all these sites were of varied origins and from different eras, although more recently it has been shown that sacred sites are linked not only by geography but also by time, so that there is in effect continuity of worship at many if not all of the locations in question.

"Today, there's a great deal of interest in these theories and it is agreed that, if there is anything in them, then there has to be a reason – a practical purpose. Some think this purpose could be linked to the science of numbers, to the movements of stars and planets and suns, to the affinity of prehistoric religions with nature, and even to the harnessing of cosmic forces for some enormously important scheme of human endeavour that is currently not understood but in the distant past was vital to the development of mankind."

This resounding piece of oratory appeared to terminate Warley's discourse and, whilst he drank coffee, I looked at him musingly. Finally I said, "Am I correct in supposing that, because you have brought up these ley-lines, you are suggesting that there was such a link between the monolith on Waterhatch Common and the ruined temple near Pataguala? And that the two children somehow travelled along that link and ended up in the jungle, adopted by leopards?"

He shrugged his shoulders. "Admit it's an explanation that fits the facts."

"But why? And how? If you'll excuse the cliché, Warley, the mind boggles. I've heard of the possibility of the transportation of matter – 'teleportation', I believe it's called – but it has never been proved. And, even if we assume the possibility (and I don't) why these children? Why that particular day and time? To what inconceivable and incalculable end?"

He shook his head. "I don't know. As I said, it's only a theory." He glanced at his watch and rose to his feet. "I must be off. Thank you so much for your hospitality and for listening to me."

Despite my invitation for him to remain, he elected to leave, but promised to return in the not too distant future. As I accompanied him to the front door, he said, "I'm sorry I have no answers to your questions. Theories such as this are notoriously difficult to prove. It could all be the most arrant nonsense."

I didn't know what to reply to that, so opened the front door without speaking. He walked away down the garden path, but at the front gate he paused, then turned and gave me a wry grin.

"But you have to admit it makes a darned good story!"

And with that he went through the gate and walked away rapidly: in a minute he had passed from my view.

I never saw him again.

VII
Fiddler's Hill

I

If you take the Winchcombe road out of Cheltenham, pass through the small but undeniably pretty village of Prestbury and then, where the main road bends round to the left, keep straight on, you will find yourself in a country lane that takes you away from the houses and eventually to Fiddler's Hill, which lies on your left, and might well be considered as a minor foothill to the majestic Cleeve Hill itself.

You may be forgiven if you fail to recognise it. The word 'hill' is something of a misnomer: 'mound' might be a more appropriate term. It is in fact not much more than a gentle grassy slope, extensive in area at the base but modest in height, possibly attaining some two hundred feet above sea-level at the summit. The latter is flat, measuring perhaps twelve yards by eight, and the smooth turf thereon is broken only by a few bushes and a single tree. Since it lies well off the lane, and within the boundaries of land owned by Mr George Parbold, of Greenacres Farm, an elderly and choleric gentleman with a marked dislike of trespassers and a predilection for carrying loaded shotguns, it is seldom populated by anything more than birds and insects, or maybe the occasional intrepid rabbit or fox.

Certainly far from impressive from a topographical point of view, it has been known as Fiddler's Hill as far back as one can remember, and is thus named on old maps, even those dating back to the eighteenth century, although in some instances it is misspelt 'Fidler's Hill'.

When I read in the local and national newspapers about the astounding events which recently took place on Fiddler's Hill, I realised with a sense of excitement that I could perhaps be on the scent of another tale. My subsequent researches into the origins of the name, and of the recent happenings in connection with the locality, have led me to a somewhat bizarre conclusion – one that I must confess I do not in the least understand.

Perhaps you will be able to make some sense out of it.

II

When I began to make enquiries as to why Fiddler's Hill was so called, I met with a surprising amount of unenlightenment. Most of my contacts in the local history group told me quite categorically that there was nothing in the records to help me and that, as far as they could see, it would be useless for me to pursue my researches. In answer to my question as to whether it might, hopefully, be a Stone Age barrow, or some other kind of burial place, they were quite scathing in their dismissal of the idea, advising me that there was no evidence to support such a theory.

However, I was not so easily deterred, and eventually my enquiries, which took me further and further afield, came up with one clue. Apparently there was some story about the naming of the hill, but all recognised authorities regarded it as so fanciful and so impossible that they did not wish to acknowledge its existence. Armed with this vague but hopeful information, I went back to my local history contacts: but most of them remained aloof and declined to help me any further – with one exception. She – more kindly than the others (possibly because she was married to a cousin of mine) – suggested I got in touch with a Mr Daniel Farquarson, who knew this preposterous story and might be persuaded to relate it to me. Accordingly I telephoned Mr Farquarson, who resided in Charlton Kings, and after a brief chat we arranged to meet in the 'Goat & Compasses' at Leckhampton the following evening. He did not seem too keen to tell me what he looked like, so I gave him a description of myself and said that I would be carrying a copy of a book entitled *Cotswold Heritage*, a recently-published book by a local author.

The next evening found me cosily ensconced in a corner seat in the crowded bar, enjoying a quiet drink as I watched the assembly drinking, chatting, arguing and playing darts. I wondered if any of them was in fact Mr Farquarson, and why it was that he was able to tell me about this strange tale, if no one else could – or would. It occurred to me that he might not be too flush money-wise and might have it in mind to seek financial reward for regaling me with some cock-and-bull story that would obviously be arrant nonsense. I decided to be stern and question his motives before committing myself to anything.

About nine o'clock the crowd at the bar seemed to part and to let through an elderly gentleman who approached me, raised his hat courteously, and enquired my name. Upon my supplying this information, he said, "I am Daniel Farquarson. I believe you are expecting me?"

I said that I was, and invited him to sit with me. I asked him if he would like a drink and he replied that a tomato juice would suit him 'down to the ground'. I obtained this for him, at the same time replenishing my glass, and as I sat down again he said, "I would very much like to smoke my pipe. Have you any great objection?"

I am a non-smoker myself and like all non-smokers do not relish sampling tobacco fumes second-hand. But the newcomer somehow impressed me and so I said nothing to discourage him. Accordingly he felt in his pockets, extracted a well-used Meerschaum pipe and a leather tobacco-pouch, and proceeded to fill one with the contents of the other.

I had referred to him as a gentleman entirely from his appearance, but his behaviour, manner and speech confirmed this initial impression. He looked to be in his early sixties, somewhat under average height, with a neatly-trimmed black beard and moustache. He blinked at me through spectacles in a very shortsighted manner. He wore an expensive alpaca overcoat and peeled off pigskin gloves before filling his pipe.

"Thank you for agreeing to meet me here," I said. "I hope you did not mind me telephoning you."

"Not in the least," he replied politely. "I am always pleased to make new acquaintances. I understand your especial interest concerns the locality known as Fiddler's Hill."

"After what happened there last week – yes. You read about it, I suppose?"

"Only a few days ago. I've been away up north. I believe you wish to write about it, and include the legend of how it came to be so called."

"I was told that you, and you alone, can enlighten me," I said. "How can this be?"

He thought for a moment, then said, "There are a number of versions. Perhaps your informant thought mine the most plausible! But, seriously, I must warn you," he paused to draw on his pipe, making the tobacco in it glow red, "it is only a story, regarded even by the most tolerant of us as apocryphal, whilst those of a more sceptical bent view it as nothing but a fanciful fabrication, not for wider publication. This is probably the reason you have not heard of it."

"Please relate it to me: I shall try to keep an open mind."

And now follows the story that Mr Farquarson recounted to me.

In the early part of the eighteenth century there lived in the tiny village of Prestbury a man called Michael O'Halloran, Irish by birth and a blacksmith by trade. The latter he plied at his forge, which is believed to have been located where the Methodist Church now stands. He was a man of low intelligence but great stature and strength, standing some six foot six in his socks, with a build to match. Had there been a spreading chestnut tree near his forge, he might well have been the model for Longfellow's poem.

Business was erratic, due probably to the quality of O'Halloran's work. But when he was employed he worked like the proverbial beaver, and sweated like the proverbial bull, so that it was necessary that in the evenings he should replenish his body fluids at one or more of the numerous hostelries in the area. It was thus that he acquired the reputation of a toper. It must also be said that his size, muscular development and Irish charm made him a firm favourite with all the ladies of easy virtue who lived roundabout, and thus he gained the additional reputation of a rake. Such pleasures cannot be indulged in without expenditure, so it follows that the Irishman was invariably empty of pocket by the end of each week. In short, he was a man of very little integrity, substance or standing.

One summer's night in 1736, O'Halloran was in the Royal Oak, imbibing ale in large quantities, his pockets more full than usual due to the fact that he had that very day been remunerated for some work done on the barns up at the Hall. When closing time was called, he was well into the third stage of his inebriety, having passed through (1) maudlin self-pity and (2) violent hostility (during which two large labourers were laid out cold and an oak settle was irreparably damaged) into (3) unbridled lechery. It was in this last mood that he staggered forth from the inn, vowing to anyone who wished to listen that he was going directly to the cottage of the Widow Beldam who, he averred, would be only too eager to invite him into her bed. This particular woman was in her late forties and well-known – even notorious – for the alacrity and speed with which she opened her legs to virtually all and sundry. However, her cottage was some distance away and, as O'Halloran stumbled away up the High Street, roughly in the right direction, his drinking cronies saw him off with laughter and jeers, whilst Matthew Stoppard, local farmer and bookmaker, accepted bets concerning the probability that he would never make it to his avowed destination. But Stoppard remembered O'Halloran's almost unlimited capacity to absorb alcohol, and he knew he was on a winner.

And, in fact, the Irishman did make it.

And at the widow's cottage he met Ferrets Mitchener.

O'Halloran, because of his size and muscular development, as well as his uncertain temper, and his inclination for other men's wives, had far more enemies than friends. However, one of the very few who might well have fallen into the latter category was Ferrets Mitchener, a small dark man of gypsy stock, who had a remarkable resemblance to one of his own ferrets, and who was engaged in the kind of profession that employed those very useful animals. In short, he was a poacher, and made a precarious living snaring rabbits, stealing chickens, and occasionally bagging the odd pheasant or partridge that abounded within the larger estates thereabouts. He lived by himself in a caravan well off the nearby lane, in the lee of a gently sloping hill, his horse tied to an elm-tree that grew adjacent to his 'van. Ferrets and Michael were just about as different as chalk and cheese, but they had similar proclivities – mostly heavy drinking and light women – and thus it was perhaps not surprising that Michael would meet him at the Beldam residence. As he approached the front door of same, his beer-blurred eyes beheld a slight figure peering into the uncurtained ground floor window, the flickering light of an oil-lamp illuminating his sharp ratty face and lecherous grin.

O'Halloran's wrath, never far from the surface, boiled up at the sight of what he took to be (and indeed was) a peeping Tom. He rushed forward and was about to lay Ferrets low with one blow of his leg-of-mutton fist when the small man turned, saw him and instinctively ducked.

" 'Old hard, 'old hard!" he gasped. "It's naught but meself, you great Irish loon – Ferrets!"

"Ferrets?" groped O'Halloran, peering down at him in the dim light shining through the grimy window. "And pwhat the Divvil may you be doin' at the Widow Beldam's?" His eyebrows drew down menacingly. "B'jasus, is it the good woman herself ye'll be after?" He balled his enormous fist and held it under the other man's hooked nose. "If it is, it's meself that'll be givin' ye the back o' me hand, ye scurvy spalpeen!"

"Huh!" responded Ferrets morosely. "You'll fare no better nor me at that caper, my fine foolish ninny. She be spoken fur tonight."

"Spoken for? Who's doin' the speaking?"

f

" 'Ave a gander through this 'ere winder, you great Irish malapert."

Michael stooped low and peered in through the window into the dimly-lit room, then straightened up, his craggy face a picture.

"You speak naught but the truth, the Divvil take the scarlet strumpet. B'jasus, I'll just be goin' in there and what I'll do to . . . "

Ferret caught his arm as he started towards the door.

"You'll do naught 'ere, you great Irish scallawag. She ain't your sole property, nor mine neither." He tugged at his companion. "But rot me if I don't 'ave a better thought in me head. I've got a firkin of good Gloster ale in me 'van what needs attention. Game?"

It was evident from the varying emotions chasing themselves across O'Halloran's heavy features that he was in two minds as to which course of action to adopt, but in the end the alcohol won and he grunted assent. The two of them moved away from the cottage and towards Ferret's 'van. It is perhaps doubtful whether the Irishman would have made it on his own, but Ferret was still fairly sober and rendered what assistance he could. They reached the 'van, and Ferrets had one foot on the lower step when he paused.

"Pwhat the Divvil ails thee?" growled O'Halloran, narrowing his eyes.

"Wheest!" exclaimed Ferrets, his long pointed ears pricking up and forwards like those of the animal after which he was named. "Bless my buttons if I can't 'ear music – and where no music should rightly be."

"Music?" scoffed the Irishman. " 'Tis your brains a-curdling, me foine feller. Pwhat sort o' music would it be then, out here and at this hour?"

"If me blighted ears don't tell me wrong, it be fiddle music what I 'ears," replied Ferrets, his dark face a portrait of wonder under the fragile moon. "But wheest a while, you great Irish layabout, and 'ear it fur yourself."

The two men were silent and still at the foot of the 'van steps. Finally Michael's eyes widened and he nodded.

"B'jasus but you're roight: 'tis fiddle music." His brows

contracted. "But pwhat the divvil would fiddle music be doin' out here and at this hour?" A look of alarm crossed his visage and he clutched at his companion. "By the howly Saint Mary, d'ye think it moight be . . . the . . . the Divvil hisself?"

Like many Irishmen of that time, O'Halloran's intrepid courage in the face of physical danger was matched by his inordinate fear of anything which he suspected might be of supernatural origin. But Ferret's character was almost precisely the opposite of this: his timidity when faced with human foes was coupled with a healthy scepticism concerning anything he didn't understand.

"The Devil, you say? 'Oo's 'e when 'e's at 'ome? The only devil you know lies inside that hulking frame of yourn, you great Irish bog-trotter." (Ferrets thus unknowingly pre-empted Freudian psychology by some two hundred years.) "But the Devil take me for a rapscallion if I knows why fiddles be a-playing like that around these parts." He listened some more. "Rot my hide, but I do believe it comes from up that hill there. What can be a-going on up there?"

He moved round the 'van and stared towards the summit of the small hill.

"I reckons I can see summat up there," he said, half to himself. "Rot my hide if I don't go up there and see what's afoot."

Ignoring O'Halloran's fearful expostulations, and evading a belated grab at his jacket, he walked to the foot of the hill and began to climb up. The Irishman, more frightened at the idea of being alone than of the consequences of climbing the hill, rushed after him.

"It's getting louder, rot me if it ain't," whispered Ferrets as they neared the flat top. "I reckon there's more'n one of 'em, too."

It was at that moment that they both halted, petrified in their tracks with fright, tongues stuck to the dry roofs of their mouths. For, as the eerie music of the unseen fiddle-players increased in volume, so the source of it slowly began to appear. Some thirty feet in front of them, on the flat grass, just above eye-level, a strange mist started to form. It thickened and swirled and coiled and, in front of the mesmerised newcomers, coalesced into several indistinct shapes. Ferrets and O'Halloran were rooted to the ground, underneath a sullen sky thick and lowering with heavy broken cloud, through which a crescent moon shone only occasionally, and watched with bulging eyes as the forms took shape – still vague and blurred at the edges, but now recognisable as three human figures crouched in a rough circle, their arms moving as if they were playing violins.

Whatever else they were, they were not of this earth.

Barely had this scene registered in the watchers' fear-numbed minds than their senses were assaulted by a further and even more horrifying development. Another mist formed in the centre of the three crouching figures and gradually it too thickened and coalesced into a recognisable shape. And as this new phenomenon became clearer, Ferrets uttered a feeble moan and clutched with palsied fingers at O'Halloran's rigid arm (the Irishman was so struck with terror that he was petrified into total immobility). The centre shape was that of a gallows – and it was occupied!

The eerie mist continued to swirl around the gallows and thicken into yet another shape, and when this latest apparition was sufficiently formed to be recognisable, a moan of fear issued from Ferret's quivering lips, whilst his face (and that of the Irishman) was as pale as the occasional gleams of moonlight that leaked through the odd rift in the cloud-cover. Hanging from the outstretched arm of the gallows was a rope, and at the end of the rope dangled the body of a man, limp and lifeless, the head bent at an impossible angle, the face contorted into a mask of agony by the rictus of violent death.

Still the two watchers were unable to force movement into their paralysed limbs. The strange unearthly music persisted, and the weird frenetic gesticulations made by the three players crouched around the gallows grew more and more grotesque, whilst the 'corpse' seemed to writhe and twist and sway in horrendous rhythm with the eerie fiddle music, almost as though it were still alive – but only just.

A full minute went by – and a moment later the shimmering blurred apparition abruptly vanished. The gallows, the corpse, the three fiddle-players, all vanished from sight, the music ceased, and the befuddled eyes of the two men beheld nothing more than the bare flat top of the hill, innocent of anything save grass and ferns and small bushes and the single tree, all silent and empty beneath the fitful moonlight.

Thus freed from the terror that had kept them rooted to the spot, with one accord Ferrets and O'Halloran turned and fled back down the slope, nor did they stop until they were both inside the 'van, shuddering with reaction and gulping down ale.

It was a long time before either of them dared venture outside. Finally Ferrets poked his head out and looked fearfully up at the top of the hill. There was nothing to be seen, only the empty hill in the moonlight.

Needless to say, neither of them dared to venture up the summit again, neither that night nor for many nights thereafter. And when the following day dawned bright and sunny, they began to doubt whether they had in fact seen or heard anything unusual. Their brains were still dulled by all the alcohol and, when they staggered out into the open air, bleary-eyed and well hung over, they looked at one another and wondered whether it had all been a hallucination or a nightmare (their brains were not equipped to understand that, whilst a hallucination may be shared, a nightmare may not). Whatever the answer, the recollection of the ignoble part they had both played in the drama made them think once, then twice and then three times as to whether they should say anything at all about the affair. Ferrets was ever close-mouthed, as befits one in his profession, whilst the Irishman was not noted for his loquacity. In the end they took a fearful oath never to reveal what they had witnessed (or thought they had witnessed) to a living soul, and sealed the bargain with several stoups of ale.

Alas, they had not reckoned on the tongue-loosening properties of the amount of ale O'Halloran was wont to absorb in an evening at the Goat and Compasses. Barely three days had elapsed before the Irishman was to be found in the bar-parlour, maudlin with drink and sobbing into his tankard (having entered well into stage one of his inebriation) in which he bemoaned his lot with loud lamentations, and called upon 'Howly Saint Patrick' to rescue him from a life full of misery and woe. He harangued his jeering laughing cronies and compared his present pitiful existence with that of the "poor feller a-danglin' from the gallows up on the hill and a-dancing to the tune played by the three fiddlers." His listeners pricked up their ears and one, bolder than the rest, pressed the drunken O'Halloran for details. As a result he and his cronies were regaled with the full story, a trifle incoherent and disconnected, but nevertheless the full story. Later that same crowd sought out Ferrets in one of his many hideouts and obtained his reluctant corroboration (extracted under threat of physical violence). The tale ran round the village like wildfire and soon spread to the surrounding countryside. By and large it was not believed, but also some were at pains to point out the surprising numbers of ways in which the two stories, given at different times and in different places, tallied. It was however talked about very freely by all the inhabitants of Prestbury and nearby villages, and soon it became quite the fashion for groups of village youths (in sufficient numbers to feel safe) to spend the night up on the flat grassy summit of the hill, hoping to experience a repetition of the visitation described so vividly by the two men.

But it never happened again.

And, in fact, so far as is known, it was never seen or heard again. But the story became woven into the fabric of village life and eventually turned into a local legend, whilst forever afterwards the locality was known as Fiddler's Hill.

III

After spending quite some time on the story Mr Farquarson had recounted to me, I embarked on a programme of investigation in an attempt to corroborate any of the details. But I met with no more success than did my predecessors. There was virtually nothing in any records to support the story. The only item that was in the least relevant was that there had undoubtedly been a smithy on the site mentioned, and the parish archives did reveal the fact that there had been people with the surname O'Halloran living in Prestbury in the eighteenth century. But there were no traces of anyone with the surname Mitchener. Furthermore, there was no record of a gallows ever having been erected on Fiddler's Hill, and no trace of any family called Beldam. Every avenue I explored came to a dead end: anything remotely like a clue led nowhere.

Needless to say, I received scant sympathy from members of the local history group, many of whom had been over the same ground before me, and on more than one occasion. Even Mr Farquarson could offer no advice as to how I should proceed: and in the end I was forced – reluctantly – to admit total defeat.

In any case, it was made all the more confusing by the sequel – the well-nigh incredible occurrence that took place up on the hill very recently, and which of course served to renew interest in both the locality and the legend. So clearly my next task is to relate what happened, and to let my readers judge for themselves.

IV

Such, unfortunately, is the state of the world today that the 'yob' culture is to be found everywhere. And it is probably true to say that it is, if anything, worse in the United Kingdom than almost anywhere else: even such a beautiful town as Cheltenham cannot escape censure in this regard.

Take for instance that appalling and depressing phenomenon, characteristic of this age of violence and promiscuous sex, known as the Devil's Disciples. This was the name applied to gangs of youths and girls who were predisposed towards mayhem and immorality, and who rode around on fast and powerful motor-bikes, wore black leather clothing, indulged in group sex without restraint, and occasionally – like lemmings – headed en masse for a town or a particular area for the sole purpose of causing as much trouble and damage as possible.

Groups of Devil's Disciples were known as 'covens' and their members, both male and female, were known by such bizarre cognomens as Big Jim, Alligator Al, Killer Duggan or Randy Rosie. Their creed was violence, their gods and goddesses the current icons of the pop music world, their characters totally devoid and bereft of morals, gentleness or charity. Yet, strange to relate, within the covens there existed a crude code of honour as strict and as rigidly enforced as any practised by exalted regiments in the British Army. One of the articles of this unwritten but irrevocable code was that, if any member of a coven was harmed or wronged by an 'outsider', his colleagues were duty-bound to take their revenge, either immediately or in due course; and until such time as that remedial action was taken, the 'stain' remained on record, as concrete as if it had been chipped out of a stone slab.

This particular coven with which we are concerned had its centre in Birmingham, and drew its members mainly from the industrial and commercial complex of which that city is the core: but some came from towns outside this sprawling conurbation, and there were in fact three who lived (or squatted) in Cheltenham (to the everlasting discredit of that town). They were two youths and a girl, known by their gang pseudonyms as 'Raper' Ron, 'Flash' Harry and 'Twice-a-night' Tracey. They were typical of their kind, sporting bizarre leather gear and arousing the baffled fury of the neighbourhood with their thunderous motor-bikes and their arrogant and immoral behaviour. And it has to be said that Tracey was possibly the most outrageous of the three. She drank to excess, abused her body with drugs, used more four letter words than any fish-porter or docker, and opened her legs to any male between the ages of puberty and senility (not to mention members of her own sex).

This sort of behaviour, practised by one who had not yet attained her twentieth birthday, was not conducive to a serene or trouble-free existence. 'Twice-a-night' Tracey was almost certainly doomed to an early demise and, before that, to a life full of conflict and not a few traumatic incidents.

One such began, for the two youths as well as for Tracey, the night they met Gypsy Dan. The three of them were in the Royal

Oak, drinking and carousing and, as usual, making a rowdy nuisance of themselves. Josh, the landlord, was too scared of any possible repercussions to throw them out, and none of the regulars were keen to take on the commitment, even if they had been able physically to do so, which was doubtful. As the empty glasses accumulated on their table, and their boisterous behaviour and abominable language grew worse and worse, Josh considered telephoning for the police, but privately he doubted whether they would be in any hurry to put in an appearance, such were the evil reputations of the three roisterers.

But then, at ten o'clock, there entered into the bar the wiry figure of Gypsy Dan, his body deceptively slim but corded with muscle, his dark eyes flicking about the smoky room, the lids half-closed with suspicion. He was served with a pint by Josh himself, who knew him as a rogue but one with a certain integrity, and normally with his pockets well-lined with cash; and it was not wise to hazard any guesses as to where it came from. Dan was carrying his drink over to an unobtrusive corner when 'Flash' Harry, barging his way unceremoniously through the throng, knocked Dan's elbow and caused him to spill half its contents.

"Watch it, sonny," growled Dan, only slightly put out. His was a volatile temperament, but it took quite a lot of provocation to set him alight.

Harry, by now well into his cups, responded with a typical obscenity, in essence inviting him to perform an act that was anatomically and physically impossible.

"And watch your filthy mouth: I don't take that kind of talk from lippy kids," the other said tartly, the fuse to his temper now smouldering.

Harry answered with a four-letter-word-laden comment which in effect cast doubt upon the other's virility, manhood and parentage. Gypsy Dan's face darkened more than its normal mahogany hue and he made a threatening movement with his fist. Harry interpreted it correctly as danger, and reacted by producing a flick-knife which he unleashed and held in his hand, palm uppermost, the business-end pointed at Dan's stomach.

"Start something, Gyppo, and see if you kin finish it," he snarled.

Whilst 'Raper' Ron and 'Twice-a-night' Tracey looked on with bleary-eyed interest, and the rest of the crowd in the bar held their breath, Josh bustled forward.

" 'Ere, you lot, pack it in. I don't want no trouble," he blustered, although the uncertainty in his voice betrayed his doubt as to whether he could handle the situation.

Neither protagonist paid him any heed, nor did the audience, who awaited developments with tankards poised halfway to their lips.

Dan's hand moved more swiftly than the eye could follow. His strong slim fingers gripped the other's wrist in a steely grip and with one rapid irresistible twist caused the knife to clatter to the wooden floor.

"Your move, sonny," he said softly.

Harry, realising that the 'honour' of the Devil's Disciples, Cheltenham branch, was at stake, and appreciating that his so-called 'mates' were going to leave it to him to sort it out, sprang at the gypsy, but he was seized in a vice-like hug and thrown bodily and humiliatingly into his chair. Dan glanced at the other two at the table. "Keep your tame monkey in order, or he'll wish he never started anything." Ron was about to react but the girl snarled, "Knock it off: you're no match for him." Her eyes were on Dan's wiry body with more than passing interest.

"He'll get over it, gypsy," she said. "Why not park your bum and have a drink with us? I reckon you and me could have some fun together, know what I mean?"

'Flash' struggled up out of his chair to attack Dan, but the girl slapped his face. "I said knock it off!" she snapped.

Dan looked at Harry with amusement. "By Christ, sonny, she's got you well and truly under her thumb, eh?"

'Raper' Ron spoke. "You'd better clear, pal, before you get carved up proper."

"You and how many others?" retorted Dan, still highly amused.

"And you can knock it off too," Tracey said to Ron. She gave Dan a smouldering look. "Well?" She glanced at his crotch. "I reckon you've got in your pants something what'll make me very happy."

"And it's staying there," said Dan. "I don't want the pox."

He walked away from them, carrying his half-empty tankard. Again Harry leapt up, ready if not willing to take the matter further, but this time it was Ron who slapped his face, causing him to fall back in his chair.

"Leave it," he commanded. "We'll do for him later."

"Yeah," whispered Tracey, her face transfigured by vicious hatred for the gypsy after his last remark. "We'll do for him later all right."

Towards midnight that same evening, three motor-cycles roared along the lane leading to Fiddler's Hill. At a certain spot, the engines cut out and the three riders coasted into a clearing in the woods fringing the lane. They set out from the clearing on foot, all three invisible in black leathers and knee-length black boots, as they kept out of the moonlight and in the deep shadows, their crouched posture full of menace. At one moment a bird flew out of a thicket at their approach and Harry spat out an obscene oath, but the others bade him keep his trap shut.

Eventually the dark bulk of the gypsy's caravan loomed up, the moonlight glinting off the roof. Light emanated from one small window, curtained with some opaque material.

"The bastard's there all right," said Ron quietly.

"Shut it!" snarled the girl in a hoarse whisper. "He's probably got ears like an effing hawk."

The three slipped silently up to the caravan and crouched below the level of the window, listening.

A murmur of voices came from within, and the three exchanged glances.

"How many, d'ye reckon?" Tracey asked Ron. She saw him shrug.

"It don't matter," whispered Harry. "Let's get in there and sort the bastard out."

Before anyone could move, they heard a giggle come from within the caravan and it began to rock on its wooden springs.

"Hey, he's got a bird in there!" ejaculated Ron. He grinned at Tracey. "No wonder he didn't want to slip you a length, baby."

Tracey's face was a picture of well-nigh insane fury.

"I'll kill the effing bastard!" she choked. "I'll squeeze his effing neck until his effing eyes pop out, and I'll break every effing bone in his body and rip him to effing shreds whilst he's still alive. And then I'll do the same to his effing floozie!"

"OK, enough talk. Let's get in there," said Ron. He smashed the door open with one violent kick from his heavy boot and the next second they were inside.

Dan and the girl – a local flibbertigibbet from the village – were on the caravan's one bed, both naked, on the verge as it were but not yet fully committed. The girl screamed, Dan lashed out with his bare feet and caught Ron full on the chest. But Harry and Tracey were on him the next moment. The girl escaped through the open door and ran away from the caravan. A homeric battle ensued, at the end of which the inevitable happened and Dan was down on the floor, his wrists and ankles securely lashed with ropes.

"What we goin' to do with the bastard?" asked Harry savagely, fingering several nasty bruises on his unprepossessing features.

Tracey made several suggestions which made the excesses of the Spanish Inquisition sound like a girl guide's picnic, and Dan's dark-skinned face paled visibly as he listened.

"Whatever we do, it mustn't be here," said Ron positively. "That effing floozie he had in here will sound the alarm. We'd better get him out of here pronto."

The two men carried the gypsy's bound figure out into the moonlight. Tracey followed them. Seeking inspiration, she looked about her and her eyes fell on Fiddler's Hill, gently flat at the summit and unoccupied save for a few bushes and a single solitary tree. One branch projected out at right-angles to the ground and this gave her an idea.

"I know what we'll do, we'll hang the bastard from that tree up there," she said triumphantly. "Then we can do what we like to him."

Her suggestion was agreed to, and the three of them climbed

the grassy slope with their writhing but helpless burden.

The naked girl had not in fact escaped from the area entirely: she had hidden in a copse of thick bushes. She was still shuddering with fright and reaction at the sudden attack, but she was still able to think logically and knew that, although she was safe, her lover was not. Although being sexually promiscuous, she had a great liking for the nut-brown and virile gypsy, so she turned and ran with desperate haste towards the nearest cottage, occupied by Mr & Mrs Devenish, their two children and numerous pet animals and birds. The arrival of the girl was later described by Tom Devenish in the bar of the Royal Oak.

"It were near enough midnight," he told his audience, which included reporters from the national and local press. "Me and the missus was asleep, kids too. We was woken up by this thunderous knocking at the door, and someone screaming – a female, it were. I took a while waking up – I'd been out in the fields till late, ye see – but the missus leaned her head out of the window to see what all the fuss was about, and of course she saw this girl standing below – bare-arsed as a coot! I got to hand it to her, though: she were able to tell the missus what it were all about, and she went down and let her in and gave her some clothes whilst I went to Jim Parson's place, what had a phone, and I phoned the police. They came along in no time at all – full marks to 'em – and as soon as they got the details they was off up Fiddler's Hill."

It only remains for me to tell what the police found up there. They parked their car at the foot, near the van, and as soon as they got out they could see something going on up at the summit. And they could hear music – fiddle music. They rushed up the hill to the flat top and, when they saw what had happened, even the most hardened among them felt physically sick, and at least one of the young men vomited up his supper.

The gypsy's naked body dangled from the projecting branch of the tree, swaying gently in the night breeze, wrists and ankles still bound, and there was blood everywhere, trickling, oozing and welling from a thousand savage cuts and slashes in his dark flesh. Surrounding this horrific sacrifice were the three Devil's

Disciples, in their leather gear, stoned out of their minds on drugs, squatting on their haunches, mumbling incoherently, and swaying and gesticulating in bizarre rhythm with eerily dissonant violin music, rising and falling with alien cadences and impossible chords, coming from a portable radio placed below and to one side of the limp dangling feet of the victim.

Later, one policeman, who knew his local history rather well, gave his opinion that, as far as he could see, it was nothing more nor less than a re-enactment of the old legend of the vision of Fiddler's Hill, although his colleagues scoffed, saying that, apart from anything else, for one thing the three on the ground had not been playing fiddles.

Splitting hairs, I call it.

Anyway, that's about it.

Oh, except for one thing. I've been told that I must be frank and mention every single item of interest appertaining to the whole affair. I haven't said anything about this last point before because – well, frankly, it can only confuse you.

It was the gypsy's name.

Dan Fidlas.

VIII

The Olde Manse

Some two or three miles south-west of Cheltenham one finds the small hamlet of Shurdington. A minute but in some ways an appealing parish, its main drawback is that it straddles the straight and busy A46 connecting Cheltenham with Stroud, Bath and the West Country.

Just outside the village, down a little-frequented side lane and well away from the main road there lay – until the beginning of this year – a large house called, simply 'THE MANSE'. It dated back to the seventeenth century and, although it did not look as large as a mansion, it boasted a fair number of rooms on the ground floor, six bedrooms on the floor above, four more above that, and a number of attics. In addition it had extensive cellars, some half-a-dozen outhouses, stabling, and garden features ranging from a rose arbour to a small maze.

It had been empty and derelict for many years, due mainly to the fact that it had been allowed to sink into such a gross state of disrepair that it would have cost enormous sums of money to put it back into any kind of habitable condition. This was not, it must be said, the first time in its career that it had been reduced to such a sad state, but on the earlier occasion – in 1905, to be precise – someone with sufficient funds had come to the rescue.

But more of that anon. In recent years of grace no such benefactor could be found and eventually, after much argument and discussion and energetic protests, the house was razed to make way for a development of new housing. And, in the grounds, buried under the floor of one of the dilapidated outhouses, was found a . . .

But I would be spoiling the finale of my story if I revealed the nature of the find in advance. So I will keep that tit-bit to the end and will now recount in detail the story of the Manse and what happened to it and its occupants almost a century ago.

Late in the year 1905, the small and peaceful village of Shurdington was stirred into unusual excitement by the news that the Manse was at long last to be occupied once more.

The old house had been empty for many years, and this lack of habitation and use had resulted in a considerable amount of decay and deterioration; even from a layman's point of view it was clearly necessary to spend a great deal of cash on it to put to rights.

The fact that it had been empty for so long was due in the main to its reputation for being haunted, a reputation which had been not one whit diminished by the circumstance that the last owner, Sir Roger Pendure, had been found beaten to death in his own bed and no assailant ever apprehended. The atmosphere surrounding the house had grown up slowly over the years, taking much time to blossom owing to the fact that it was rooted in a very few instances of abnormal activity and all these insubstantial and unproven.

No ghosts had ever been seen. There had been stories of invisible presences in the rooms, and there had been disturbances which could be attributed to poltergeist activity but which could equally be explained by more mundane circumstances. It was said that floorboards had creaked where no human foot had trod; that ornaments had fallen from shelves entirely of their own volition; that strange whistlings, pipings and dronings had been heard but no visible source perceived; that there had been inexplicable draughts where no windows or doors were open. But all efforts to prove the existence of anything supernatural in connection with these events (if they had occurred, which not a few doubted) were unsuccessful. One attempt to exorcise an alleged unhappy and earthbound spirit had had no apparent effect. The result was that by the year of which I speak – 1905 – the house was much neglected and run down through disuse, and it was obvious that so much would be needed to reclaim it as a residence that it was doubtful if it would ever be lived in again.

Thus it was that, in November of that year, when it was learned that the Manse was to be fully restored and refurbished ready for use, many of the villagers were at first dubious. It had not seemed possible that they would ever again see lights at the windows, or carriages once more in the drive. But later it became known that the purchaser was a rich banker from the USA who – presumably – had access to virtually unlimited funds. Still later it was understood that the said banker was keen to divide his time between his palatial home in Newport, Rhode Island, and a more traditional residence situated somewhere in the ancient land from which his forebears had emigrated in the dim and distant past, when the eastern seaboard of North America was being colonised by men and women from the British Isles driven out by religious persecution. Later it was learned that Mr Samuel P. Smith, executive president of the First Federal Bank of America, had no idea from which part of the UK his ancestors had sprung (his name of course providing no clue whatsoever) and he had picked Shurdington for its picturesque rurality and its proximity to Cheltenham and Bath, both of which he knew and liked.

As soon as hordes of workmen descended on the Manse, swarmed all over its dilapidated exterior, and penetrated (admittedly a trifle apprehensively) into the gloomy and cobwebbed recesses of the interior, the locals realised that little or no expense was being spared. Work went on day after day, week after week, and, since Mr Smith had ordered that the house must be restored to its original appearance and condition (apart from updating the plumbing and heating arrangements) gradually the house resumed the appearance it had once proudly displayed to the world.

Towards the end of April, 1906, the owner, his family and certain members of the staff moved in. The new squire of

Shurdington turned out to be a man in his late forties, of average height and corpulent build, with a richly rubicund visage that hinted at high blood pressure: his appearance was not improved by a pair of metal-rimmed spectacles. He was a widower and had two children, a daughter aged 21 with the name Barbara, and a son aged 13 called Sam Junior.

Accompanying them from the States were two men: a private secretary named Clark Fussberger who was young, slim and studious in demeanour, and a butler-cum-valet called William Dietz who was of middle age, also slim, but with an excessively pale face. This transatlantic nucleus was rapidly augmented from the neighbouring houses by Mrs McDade the housekeeper, Mrs Tennyson the cook, Elizabeth Pocock, parlour-maid, and Mary Connolly, kitchen-maid. Later they were joined by George Wibley, gardener, the only one among the staff who did not live in.

This assorted assemblage of people settled down together in the newly refurbished Manse and in a creditably short space of time welded themselves into a more-or-less harmonious household. Samuel P. Smith continued to conduct his business affairs from a study on the ground floor, with the aid of several of the new-fangled telephones that were just becoming popular in England, and with the quiet and able assistance of Clark Fussberger. The latter proceeded to belie his studious appearance by taking up with not a few of the more comely and necessarily-eligible spinsters of the neighbourhood (but not all at the same time, of course) and his dark good looks and slim figure caused flutters in many a feminine bosom, so that he was much sought after for dinners and parties by those local matrons keen to have their nubile daughters taken off their hands.

In much the same way the young men of the area were smitten by the charms of Barbara Smith. She was a redhead who had been blessed by beauty of face and figure that was as close to perfection as any male could desire, and she enhanced her loveliness with a light and modern vivacity, and a keen knowledge of the world around her, that was both a revelation and a reproach to the more sheltered young ladies living nearby.

William Dietz the butler-cum-valet remained something of an enigma. He spent most of what little time he had either within the Manse, or taking long walks in the countryside, and he made no contacts with the local populace. It was understood that he was very skilful at chess and gave his employer a hard game most evenings. It was also rumoured that he was writing a book of his memoirs, although no confirmation of this could be obtained.

Mrs McDade aroused the baffled rage, albeit also the reluctant admiration, of many of the local merchants and shopkeepers, by frequent demonstrations of her ability to choose the best quality merchandise and barter for the lowest prices. And the produce which she had delivered to the Manse were turned into masterpieces of the culinary art by Mrs Tennyson, whose homely appearance belied her talents as a provider of menus that would not have disgraced the best restaurant in London.

Sam Junior, the son, was unhappy at being wrested away from his friends and school in Patience, Rhode Island and, after one or two escapades, his father sent him to one of the better public schools in England, where he spent a couple of undistinguished months (notable in the main for his lack of any progress at his studies, and his complete failure to understand or play cricket, soccer and rugby) before returning home for the summer vacation.

It was on the second night of that vacation that the first of a number of inexplicable phenomena occurred.

The boy had spent much of his spare time at the school constructing a sailboat from wood, and had brought it home to finish rigging it with the aid of materials obtained, hopefully, from Mrs McDade. It was now completed and had pride of place on the narrow ledge above the fireplace in his bedroom on the first floor, and he had given strict instructions, particularly to Elizabeth, that it should not be touched by ANYONE.

It was about three in the morning when Sam Junior was woken up by a thud. He sat up in bed. Moonlight filtered through a chink in the curtains and he looked round the room to see if anything was amiss. At first he spotted nothing and was about to settle down to sleep again when he saw the patch of moonlight on the wall immediately above the mantelpiece.

No boat!

He jumped out of bed, now fully awake, and found his model on the hearth-rug, the hull intact but the masts broken and the rigging tangled and some ornamental projections snapped off.

He was pardonably displeased, but his father displayed little sympathy when the incident was related to him, stating that in his opinion the boy must have positioned the model precariously. Sam Junior denied this, pointing out that the shelf was some six inches wide and that it did not slope towards the floor. His father remained unconvinced, and only laughed at the boy's suggestion that a mouse might have run along the shelf and knocked the boat from its perch. Barbara was equally scathing about the idea, which also met with opposition from Mrs McDade, who stated with considerable vehemence and righteous indignation that there were no mice in *her* establishment.

The occurrence was soon forgotten, nor was it linked to further unexplainable happenings which took place three nights later. Mr Smith slept in a spacious room along the corridor leading from the top of the sweeping staircase. He had an unusually large bed, imported from the USA. Next to the bed was a heavy cabinet on which reposed the family Bible (he was a devoutly religious man), a candle-stick with candle and matches, and a glass carafe with a glass tumbler inverted over the neck to protect the water contained therein from the dust in the atmosphere. He went to his room late on this occasion – well after midnight – and when he went to his bed he discovered the carafe on the floor, its contents drained into the carpet. There was no way in which it could have happened by accident, as *the tumbler was still on the cabinet top, and still in its inverted position.*

Although he was not normally an irascible man, this seemed to him to be a wanton and wicked prank that needed immediate action. Naturally he suspected his son and went to the boy's room to confront him, only to find the boy apparently fast asleep: and the door of his wardrobe wide open and every article of clothing normally contained therein lying scattered about the floor and some even on the boy's bed.

As soon as he was aroused and made aware of the two events, Sam Junior vehemently denied all knowledge of them, and such was his earnestness that his father was inclined to accept his tearful word. He was glad that he had done so, for when he returned to his room he found the family Bible on the floor quite a distance from the bed, opened, *and a number of pages torn out.* This was confounding: it had not been so when he left the room, in which case his son could not have been responsible.

But if not Sam Junior, then who? Mr Smith alerted Dietz, who was in the process of locking up downstairs, and the butler roused the rest of the staff and conducted a searching enquiry there and then. But nothing emerged. Everyone strongly denied having any part in the three mishaps and in truth Mr Smith could hardly suspect any of them, save possibly the Irish kitchen-maid, who had a somewhat irreverent tongue-in-cheek sense of humour that had got her into trouble before. But Elizabeth Pocock, who shared a small attic-room with Mary Connolly, swore on the Bible that neither of them had left their room since retiring at 11.30pm.

The mystery remained unsolved: and no doubt the matter would have faded from memory had no further untoward incidents occurred. But the very next evening Mrs McDade was descending the main staircase after checking the bedrooms to make sure that Elizabeth had prepared them for the night when she was struck on the shoulder by a heavy object which then shattered and fell in pieces on the stairs. Both shocked and hurt, she cried out, staggered, and was obliged to catch hold of the banisters for support. The noise brought William Dietz from the lower hall and Mr Smith from his study, and together they ran up the staircase to render assistance. However, Mrs McDade was a woman strong both of body and character and within minutes she was able to assure them that she was comparatively unharmed, except that her shoulder-blade was very painful as a result of the impact: later she reported a large contusion in that area.

Their attention then turned to the cause of the trouble. The many small pieces of the missile were gathered together and it was soon apparent that they were the shards of a porcelain vase some eighteen inches high, a product of the renowned factory at Limoges, France, executed in the likeness of a Chinese vase of the T'ang dynasty, and worth in the region of £500. It had stood in a niche in the wall at the head of the stairs. The three climbed to the top of the staircase and it soon became apparent that the incident could in no sense be an accident: the only way in which the vase could have travelled from the niche to the shoulder of Mrs McDade halfway down the stairs was by projection. Somebody, averred Dietz, must have deliberately thrown it at the housekeeper. The question was: who? Mr Smith, very much disturbed by this seemingly unwarranted attack on his strict but efficient housekeeper, conducted an immediate investigation which only served to deepen the mystery. At the time of the occurrence, Sam Junior – the most likely of a number of extremely unlikely candidates – was in bed and apparently asleep: his father had to shake him very vigorously to wake him up. Barbara had been taking a bath, attended by Elizabeth: Mrs Tennyson (as though anyone could suspect her!) was resting in the kitchen after her labours in connection with the evening meal and talking to Mary Connolly, who was in the closing stages of washing up; Clark Fussberger was out for the evening; Wibley, the gardener, had long since gone home. Unless Sam Junior had perpetrated the outrage, and had feigned sleep when his father came into his room to wake him, the identity of the attacker remained unknown: and Mr Smith, who was sharply intelligent and not easily deluded, as well as being well aware of his son's character defects, was prepared to swear that Sam Junior had been firmly asleep when the attempt was made to rouse him. In any case he found it impossible to believe that his son would not only cause harm to a person of whom he was very fond but also destroy an object of considerable value to his father: it was just not his nature to do such a thing.

And so it remained an enigma, to be added to the others. But the very next day Ossa was piled on Pelion (as Virgil would have it) as another conundrum was joined to those that had gone before. They were all seated at dinner in the dining-hall, and Elizabeth was conveying a large tureen of boiled potatoes to the table, when the French windows were abruptly assailed by a veritable shower of missiles which rattled and banged against the glass, causing panes to crack and shatter. All the diners were startled, and Elizabeth shrieked and dropped the tureen, which smashed at her feet and deposited boiled potato all over the Persian carpet. Fortunately the heavy brocade curtains had been drawn across prior to the meal and this circumstance not only muffled the noise of the impact and the breaking of the panes of glass but also protected the diners from the missiles themselves and from the showers of glass splinters. The attack continued for some minutes, during which many more panes of glass were broken, and it was observed that the curtains billowed out sharply on several occasions, testifying to the weight and force of the attack. When it seemed that at last the frightening onslaught had finished, Mr Smith and Sam Junior went to the windows, pulled back the curtains and gazed upon a scene of damage and chaos. Nearly every pane of glass in the French windows was shattered or cracked, and the floor was littered with hundreds of stones, varying in size from tiny round pebbles to jagged rocks the size of a man's fist.

Mr Smith sent Barbara for his shotgun and, whilst he waited, William Dietz appeared and was horrified at what he saw. Barbara returned with the gun and a lantern thoughtfully provided by an alert Mrs McDade. Mr Smith gripped his gun purposefully, Dietz took charge of the lantern, and the two men stepped cautiously out onto the terrace. It was dark and silent in the huge garden. The rays of the lantern illuminated the stone balustrade and some of the sunken lawn beyond. Of intruders there was no sign. Growing bolder, the two men conducted a search of the grounds, but no trace of any unauthorised persons could be found and in the end Mr Smith sent Mary Connolly for the local police. They answered the call with creditable speed and after a close inspection of the missiles and the garden could offer no explanation. The ground was dry, and any possible 'sign' was likely to have been obliterated by the searchers. The police inspector suggested that the attack must have been the work either of a complete lunatic or of someone with a grudge against one or more members of the household. He inclined to the latter view, as there was little doubt that the act of vandalism had been premeditated. This was deduced from the fact that the majority of the stones were not from the garden and must therefore have been carried to the house by the assailant. He promised to keep working on the case.

Thus was one more mystery added to the others.

Many were the discussions among the family and their staff in connection with these several incidents, but no one came up with a satisfactory explanation. It was Mary Connolly who happened to mention, one evening in the servants' quarters, that perhaps the cause was not wholly natural. Her actual words were, "Oh, 'tis frightened I am indeed, Mrs Tennyson: it ain't due to anythin' natural, you mark my words. There be some kind av horrid hobgoblin in this house, interferin' wid our comfort of mind and body, you see if I'm not right!" She was overheard by William Dietz, who told her not to be so silly, but Mary's words caused Mrs Tennyson to recall the fact, forgotten by some members of the household, that the Manse had a reputation for being haunted. The cook was a superstitious woman and in mortal dread of anything the least bit supernatural. Her fears were shared, surprisingly enough, by Elizabeth Pocock. These two spent much time talking amongst themselves, in hushed tones, gradually augmenting the alarm they now felt, which alarm was not in the least abated when Mrs McDade poured contemptuous and forthright ridicule upon their fancies.

Eventually William Dietz told Mr Smith what some of the servants were saying below stairs. The latter – not only a hard-headed financier but also an American – reacted with scepticism tinged with anger, and he told Dietz that if any member of his staff repeated such rubbish outside the house, he or she would be instantly dismissed. This had the effect of quelling the mutterings from below stairs, and in fact a reduction of tension was brought about by the fact that no further incidents happened for several weeks.

But then they restarted – with a vengeance.

One warm summer's night the entire household was awakened

by screams emanating from the top floor. They were loud, shrill and ear-piercing, and were uttered by more than one voice, and female at that. Dietz and Mrs McDade were soon out of their bedrooms, night-robes hastily donned and lighted candles in hand. As they stared at one another in the flickering light, wondering from which direction the noise was coming, they heard a door open violently, and the next moment Mary Connolly appeared round a bend in the corridor. She wore only her nightdress, her hair was in wild disarray, and her eyes were dilated with terror. Behind her, the corridor rang with renewed screams.

"Oh howly mother av Mary, please help!" she cried with pitiful appeal in her voice and gestures. "Elizabeth's havin' a fit, so she is. There's been a man in our room – oh Jesus help me."

Mrs McDade quietened the girl down and then led the way round the bend and into the room shared by the two girls. They found the parlour-maid on her bed, the covers thrown back, and her body arching and writhing as she screamed hysterically. Since the girl's nightgown was disarranged in an unseemly fashion, Mrs McDade ordered Dietz out of the room whilst she and Mary – now comparatively calm and very co-operative – attended to the unfortunate Elizabeth. That they were successful was shown by the fact that the screaming stopped almost at once. As the butler waited outside, he was joined by Mrs Tennyson, her ample figure wrapped in a blanket, making querulous complaints about the uproar. A few minutes later Mr Smith appeared, clad in a resplendently coloured dressing-gown, demanding angrily to know why his repose had been so rudely shattered. Dietz attempted some kind of explanation, but it was not until the bedroom door opened and Mrs McDade appeared to announce that Elizabeth was now reasonably rational and ready to answer questions that his curiosity was to be satisfied.

After a patient cross-examination conducted by Dietz, with Mr Smith as judge and Mrs McDade holding what was in effect a watching brief, it became clear that the upheaval had been caused by an intruder, although at no time had anyone been actually seen. Mary had woken up first and had for a moment lain still, wondering why she had returned to consciousness. Then, suddenly, *she felt stealthy fingers take hold of her hand.* Frozen with fear and thus unable to move, she had been powerless to prevent the experience being repeated. "Loike the divvil himself had got a-hould av me," she told them, shuddering at the recollection. The third time it happened she gasped aloud with terror and, as though this released the paralysis affecting her limbs, she scrambled madly out of bed. Elizabeth woke up at once and, yawning, listened to Mary stammering out her story, but she was tired and the moonlight flooding in through the uncurtained window showed the room to be untenanted save for themselves. However, the parlour-maid left her bed, lit a candle, and together they searched the room, but to no avail. The door was shut, so it was hardly likely that any intruder had escaped that way. Mary finally decided that it must have been a mouse, whilst Elizabeth inclined to the theory that it was all due to a nightmare, due perhaps to too much supper.

Accordingly they resumed their beds, Elizabeth blew out the candle flame, and they settled down to sleep once more. But barely had a few minutes elapsed when Elizabeth felt *her* right hand seized. Like Mary earlier, she froze with fright, and within seconds her left wrist was taken in a firm grip. Total paralysis held her as fast as the unseen hands, and she could neither move nor speak. Then – and in the retelling her voice trembled – a similar hold was applied to both of her ankles. She was held fast – *by no less than four hands!* She described the grasp on her wrists and ankles as cold but firm, and far from ghostly, except that moonlight entering through an uncurtained window showed no one present. Almost out of her wits she fought to overcome her paralysis and finally managed to let out a scream. At once her limbs were released and the instant she was freed she scrambled from her bed, still screaming. This woke Mary up and she tried to calm her friend, but the latter became hysterical and collapsed onto her bed in a fit, whereupon the Irish maid ran out of the room to summon assistance.

It must be confessed that the three listeners found it difficult to believe the stories told by the two still-shuddering girls, and questions were asked about cheese suppers, and illicit hoards of gin, and the incidence of nightmares among young girls. But both females stuck stoutly to their tales, vowing that it was all true and not a product of their disordered digestions or vivid imaginations, and even Mr Smith agreed that their sincerity and earnestness seemed genuine. In the end he ordered them back to bed whilst he, Dietz and Fussberger, who had by then appeared on the scene, searched the whole house. Of course, no intruder or trace of one was found, whilst all fastenings remained secure and no windows or doors had been forced.

Thus ended a night which produced a spate of discussions among the staff over the next few days: but with all this talk no fresh clues or possible explanations emerged. Dietz was privately beginning to wonder if the rumours concerning the house being haunted were perhaps not mere wives' tales, but Mrs McDade scoffed at any suggestion that supernatural forces were involved, and Dietz dared not mention his doubts to his employer.

But two nights later his private fears were confirmed, and even the most hardened sceptics within the house were obliged to review their opinions.

The incident occurred in the evening, just before dinner. At the time Mr Smith was in his study, working on business matters; Sam Junior was in the music room at the Bluthner grand piano, practising his scales; Fussberger and Dietz were in the library, sorting out books to go on the shelves; Mrs McDade and Elizabeth were in the dining-room, preparing the table for dinner; and Mrs Tennyson and Mary were down in the kitchen, in the final stages of preparing the meal.

Suddenly the comparative silence of the house was broken by a high-pitched piping sound, reminiscent of the playing of a flute. It was not loud – in fact it sounded muffled, as though heard through a thick wall – yet it was subsequently ascertained that everyone in the house had heard it as soon as it had started, and moreover each person thought that it came from the room next to the one they were in.

As it continued, the members of the household began to assemble. Mr Smith, unable to concentrate on his paperwork, emerged from his study – to find Fussberger and Dietz already in the hall, their ears cocked and expressions of puzzlement on their faces. As the three of them discussed the phenomenon, not one of them able to pinpoint the source or explain the noise, Sam Junior erupted from the music-room complaining that it made nonsense of his scales, whilst Mrs McDade and Elizabeth appeared from the dining-room with questions in their eyes.

The fluting continued – a strange high wailing sound that frequently and erratically changed both pitch and tone, resulting in a very eerie and indeed alien music – and Mr Smith sent Dietz down to the kitchen to make enquiries. The latter returned to say that it was no louder (or softer) below stairs, and that the two in the kitchen were as baffled by it as the rest were, as well as being very uneasy and half-convinced that the origin was supernatural and therefore somehow menacing.

Barbara then appeared at the top of the stairs, asking who was playing the flute. Her father called up to her, asking if the noise seemed to come from the upper regions of the house, and she replied that it did. As a result, the eight people in the hall (Mrs Tennyson and Mary having joined them) made a concerted move towards the foot of the stairway.

At that precise moment Barbara screamed, "Help, oh help! Something has got hold of my arms."

There was a dash up the stairs, Sam Junior and Fussberger in the lead. As they reached the top, they saw that Barbara was standing in a rigid position, her face drained of blood, her eyes starting from their sockets. Her arms were pressed tightly to her sides and she was immobile, as though she were being physically restrained: yet, as far as they could see, she was alone.

As they ran towards her, her body suddenly relaxed, her eyes rolled upwards and without a sound she fell to the floor and lay inert. They all gathered round her, but Mrs McDade quickly took charge and, after a brief examination, announced that all was well: the girl had merely fainted.

As the two elderly women attended to the pale and trembling Barbara, Mr Smith addressed his son and his secretary.

"Did either of you see anyone near her?" he asked.

Both shook their heads.

"I'll stake my life there was no one within six yards of your daughter, sir," answered Fussberger earnestly, and Sam Junior agreed.

"Extraordinary," muttered Mr Smith, more to himself than to anyone present. "She shouted that she was being held." He looked at the others. "Clearly there is something amiss in this house, but what can it be?"

"As you are aware, sir, it is alleged to be haunted . . . " began Dietz, but he was summarily interrupted by his employer.

"Do not talk nonsense, Dietz. If you are a God-fearing man, and you would not be in my household if you were not, you will not believe in such claptrap. There *must* be some rational explanation for all these occurrences and I can assure you that whoever *is* found to be . . . "

"Oh – look!" yelled Sam Junior.

He pointed a quivering finger along the shadowy corridor which led past the top of the stairs and past bedroom doors towards the rear of the house. Those with him followed the direction of his pointing finger with their eyes and beheld a startling sight. The floor-boards some five or six yards from them moved, depressing slightly as though a heavy person had placed his foot upon them; the movement was accompanied by a creaking noise. The next moment the boards returned to their normal position, but a similar thing happened a few feet further on, into the shadows where the light barely penetrated. A moment later a similar phenomenon occurred several feet beyond. It was as if someone – or something – of uncommon weight was walking slowly away from them.

Sam Junior was the first to recover from the shock with which they had all been afflicted. Uttering a whoop, he dashed along the corridor in the direction the depressions were travelling, and Fussberger and Dietz followed him. As they reached a bend in the corridor, they almost stumbled over the boy, who lay sprawled out on the floor.

"I – I bumped into something," he muttered dazedly as they helped him to his feet.

"What sort of something?" queried Dietz, as Fussberger disappeared round the bend into the darkness beyond.

"I don't know," muttered Sam, clearly shaken by his experience. As his father came up, he said, "Something big . . . big and . . . and soft and . . . alive." His face was pale and he was obviously very shaken.

Fussberger returned to say that he had found nothing, but his search had been hampered by lack of light. He and Dietz procured lighted candles and they went round the bend in the corridor again. Mr Smith consoled his scared son as well as he could, but he was now beginning to wonder if his resolute determination to ignore paranormal explanations for all these bizarre occurrences was perhaps a little too dogmatic. He had seen the floor-boards sink and recover with his own eyes and despite his pragmatism he could not imagine the sort of trickery that could produce such results and he could find no answers to the questions that besieged his troubled mind.

Dietz and Fussberger returned to tell him that they had found nothing and the search was called off. Barbara recovered rapidly and attended the evening meal and there were no further alarms that night.

But the following night it all came to a head . . .

Once again Mr Smith was in his study, engaged on some important work prior to a meeting in London the following day. It was around midnight and, of the rest of the household, only William Dietz was awake. He had locked up and was in his bedroom preparing for the night.

Mr Smith glanced up from his papers. Some unusual sound had reached his ears. A second later he realised that it was that damned elusive piping noise again. As he identified it in his mind, so it seemed to grow louder. Yet it was, as it had been the night before, muffled as though through a blanket. It gradually invaded his brain with insidious penetration, a strange haunting high-pitched ululation that filled the study and came from a direction he could not identify.

He had spent some time earlier that day deciding what to do if the experience of the previous night repeated itself, and now he acted. He rose to his feet, picked up the shotgun he placed against the wall, loaded both barrels and went out into the hall. The wailing sound was still audible, the source still impossible to determine: it occupied the hall just as it had filled the study and the eerie music was in the air all about him.

He spent a few fruitless moments endeavouring to locate the origin of the sound, but was interrupted by a shrill yet muffled scream from upstairs. He gripped his gun and hastened up the stairs as fast as he could, his progress accelerated by several more screams. At the top he was met by his son in night-clothes, rubbing his eyes.

"Father, it came from Barbara's room!" he exclaimed, his face again pale.

At that moment two things happened. Dietz appeared at the far end of the passage, in dressing-gown and slippers. He held up a lighted candle and his face was questioning. Barbara's bedroom door burst open and she herself appeared, clad only in her nightgown, her hair dishevelled and her eyes wide with terror.

"It . . . it was in here," she said in a choked voice. "It . . . it touched me . . . "

She collapsed, just as Mrs McDade appeared, wrapped in a voluminous gown. As the indispensable and indefatigable housekeeper hurried to the girl's assistance, Sam Junior shouted a warning. He pointed, and once again they witnessed the amazing spectacle of the floor-boards sinking and rising again, but more rapidly this time, indicating the movement of someone (or something) excessively weighty along the corridor. And it was heading directly for the butler. The next moment Dietz staggered back against the wall, just as though he had been given a violent push.

Clark Fussberger appeared, gowned and slippered, bearing a lighted candle in one hand and a pistol in the other. He took in the situation at a glance and shouted to Mr Smith, "Come on, sir, we've got him this time." The two men hurried along the corridor, round the bend, and towards the foot of the rear stairway. Fussberger discharged his pistol, but there was no visible target at which to aim, and nothing happened. But the next minute they heard creaking noises from the back stairs and their goggling eyes beheld the ancient wooden steps bending in the centre, one after the other, in an upwards direction. Fussberger reached the foot of the stairs first and, reloading his pistol, he fired upwards.

Afterwards he found it somewhat difficult, despite his education, to describe exactly what happened.

"That damned fluting stopped at once," he said after due consideration. "And I experienced . . . well, an extraordinary sensation . . . totally inexplicable . . . as though . . . as though time itself had come to a full stop . . . as though everything had ceased to move, to breathe, even to exist. It happened for only a very brief moment, then the world started to turn again: Mr Smith came up behind me and asked me what had occurred: and when I told him we climbed the stairs together . . . to find . . . "

"Yes?"

"Not a thing," said Fussberger with instinctive drama.

"Not anything at all?"

"Well, perhaps that is not quite true. Scattered over several of the stairs were drops of a dark red liquid. It had the appearance of blood."

"And what was it?"

Fussberger shrugged. "Who can tell? It dried rapidly and quickly disappeared. One would have needed to be a professor of chemistry to be able to say. My knowledge does not encompass such matters."

It so happened that the incident I have just related was in fact the last abnormal occurrence at the Manse. Soon afterwards Sam Junior went back to his school, but whether this was a co-incidence or not will never be known. The rest of the household continued to live at the Manse without any further interruption to their ordered lives, but this state of affairs lasted only until the following year, because in early spring Mr Smith was recalled to America and from there he was sent to Canada to be chief executive of his company's many branches in that dominion. His family joined him, and the Manse was sold to Sir Kenneth Albright from London, who lived in it with his large family for many subsequent years without any supernatural events disturbing their calm and settled lives.

Most of the household who had been resident at the Manse during Mr Smith's time went to America with him: the others faded into the background.

One who did not do either of these things was Clark Fussberger. There were two reasons for this. He had become engaged to Priscilla, the only daughter of a well-to-do merchant with a thriving business in Gloucester (and other towns): and he was particularly keen to undertake an investigation into the mysterious events that had occurred, within the space of a few weeks, at the Manse. He was not only well-educated: like most products of American universities, he had a mind that was wide open to all possibilities, natural or otherwise, and he was moreover totally without prejudice. This desirable attribute was coupled with a great deal of inquisitiveness concerning the world about him, amounting (as he once said) to an itch that just *had* to be scratched.

Accordingly, once it was clear that his future, as husband to Priscilla and prospective son-in-law to the wealthy (and aged) merchant, was assured, he rented a small house in Gloucester, took on a manservant and proceeded with his enquiries.

Almost immediately he realised that it was not going to be as easy as he had at first thought. The many strange happenings at the Manse prior to its occupation by Mr Smith et al., were well-known but little documented. Most of them had been passed down the years by word of mouth, and only a few committed to paper, usually in the form of correspondence or diaries. Fussberger read up all he could, asked innumerable questions of innumerable people, made many journeys hither and thither, and spent a lot of time and burnt a lot of 'midnight oil' in writing up his notes and correlating his findings.

After several months of endeavour, both mental and physical, he paused to review his progress to date and, although admitting that his labours had not been entirely in vain, nevertheless declared his dissatisfaction at the lack of any real progress. He talked it over with Priscilla, who was surprisingly sympathetic to his cause (subsequently making him an affectionate and truly supportive wife) and she established that he had at least arrived at certain interesting conclusions.

Firstly, he was certain that the many supernormal events that had occurred at the house were similar to those which in general are laid to the charge of mischievous and, in some cases, malicious spirits known as poltergeists. This is a German word, meaning spirits that cause an uproar, and whereas in olden days they were regarded as falling within the province of witchcraft, latterly there has been a change of viewpoint, and poltergeists were now thought to be – to coin a phrase – pranksters of the supernatural. It can be argued that, of all the supernormal beings that our ancestors believed inhabited the world beyond our five senses, poltergeists are perhaps the only group still able to claim some credence. It seemed to Fussberger that, if all the events at the Manse were to be laid at the door of non-temporal beings, a poltergeist was most likely to be the culprit.

Secondly, the cause had to be rooted in the dim and distant past, evidenced by the tales of unusual happenings to people living in the house long before Mr Smith and his entourage took it over.

Thirdly, the most common theme to most of the occurrences – including many that had happened centuries before – was the sound of the phantom piper playing on his infernal and ghostly instrument.

After discussions with certain learned persons in the area, Fussberger decided to concentrate his efforts on the last-named factor. He soon discovered that there were a number of musical instruments capable of sounding like a flute, but that the one most commonly in use in the olden days was a fife, popular as part of the fife-and-drum bands in the British Army. He paid a visit to a well-known musical college and persuaded someone to play the fife to him, instantly recognising the sound it made as similar to that heard at the Manse. Encouraged by this discovery, he went to the London headquarters of the College of Military Music and spent several days talking to the curator. As a result, he was able to go to the British Museum and pore over certain ancient tomes, which in turn led him to a series of pamphlets written in the seventeenth century by the Reverend Barnaby Hutchinson, assistant chaplain to Bishop Ogden and a fellow of the Royal Society, and in particular to one written in 1685 entitled 'A True Account of the Strange Affair of the Gloucestershire Piper'.

Success was his at last, because this turned out to be nothing more nor less than a record of the investigations carried out by the Reverend Hutchinson into a sequence of baffling incidents that took place at the home of one Matthew Soames, a magistrate of Shurdington, Gloucestershire, from July 1662 to August 1663.

It all began, seemingly, on the 14th July 1662, when a man called Joseph Smith was arrested for stealing chickens from a local farmer. Smith was a vagrant who went about the countryside performing at fairs, indulging in sundry feats of country entertainment, such as cavorting in a fool's habit, tricks with goose's eggs and coins of the realm, multiple hand-springs, eating fire, and other such-like amusements. Joseph had been a flute player in a regimental fife-and-drum band and the magistrate who tried him sent him to gaol for six months and confiscated his flute, taking it home with him as a gift for his young daughter.

From that apparently unimportant event sprang a chain of abnormal occurrences at the Soames' house. According to the Reverend Hutchinson, the occupants began to the hear the ghostly playing of a flute, usually at night when they were about to go to sleep. For the first few weeks the eerie piping was heard only outside the walls, but later it penetrated through the walls and was heard in many of the rooms and passages, especially in Martha's chamber (where the flute was kept, in a cupboard). Because of this harassment, and because his daughter suffered with nervous debility as a result, Matthew Soames removed the flute and had it concealed in an outhouse. But the noises continued.

One late afternoon, on the 26th August 1662, the piping was especially loud and seemed to emanate from the daughter's room. Several servants entered the room and, deciding that the noise emanated from the cupboard where the flute had been secreted, opened the door. They were petrified to see, within the dark interior, the box wherein was stored the flute lift itself from the shelf where it had stood and float upwards. One of the men, bolder than his companions, in a none-too-steady voice bade the box "Begone!" whereupon it shivered and then slowly swivelled and moved towards him in a most menacing fashion. He seized it and at once there commenced a battle of strength between the box and the manservant, who undoubtedly showed great courage. According to witnesses, there was a great struggle which lasted some minutes, but at last the box seemed to lose the will to carry on and fell to the floor. As the Reverend Hutchinson took pains to note, "Three other servants were in the room at the same time and clearly observed all that took place, and moreover swore on the Good Book that it was so."

The daughter was much distraught and quickly moved to another bedroom, but the disturbances still plagued her, and she was further troubled by renewed pipings in the room, and her hair plucked by unseen hands, and eventually her father sent her away to relatives in Essex, where it was reported that she was no longer troubled.

But in the Soames' household the phenomena continued and now the centre of attention appeared to be the male servant, by name John Winkler, who had showed much bravery on an earlier occasion. He was a strong man of steady habits and sober conversation, but he showed great grit when, during the night, and for several nights thereafter, his bedclothes were pulled slowly from his bed, so that he was obliged to tug at them to retain them: and sometimes they were removed by a great force and thrown to the floor. And now and then he was held as though seized by invisible, and very cold, hands but found that when he was able to release his arms sufficiently to flay them about him, he could find no one present and the honest man was much perplexed thereby.

On a separate occasion he was in another room when the light seemed to fade, and he saw movements in a darkened corner by an open door that, according to him, were "not as they should be." He fired a pistol into the midst of the commotion, but there was no visible reaction, except that afterwards drops of blood were found in the corner and on the floor nearby.

When Joseph Smith was first committed to Salisbury Gaol, he was placed in a cell by himself. But soon he was allocated a cell-mate, an itinerant pedlar named Nathan Crum, who had been found guilty of harassing a farmer's wife whilst her husband was away at market. Joseph soon discovered that Nathan was from the village of Shurdington, and he therefore asked the newcomer if he knew of any 'disturbances' at a house in that hamlet. The man replied that there had been rumours of such in the several hostelries in the area, and what did Joseph know about it? Joseph then said with grim satisfaction that he knew a lot about it and added that he had 'troubled' the owner of the house, and all his kin, to the utmost of his abilities, on diverse occasions and at diverse times, so that he and his might never again rest in peace until he had reaped his just desserts for his wickedness.

When Joseph Smith was finally released from gaol, in January 1663, he found his way back to Gloucestershire, but it was not long before he was in trouble again. Having no means of support, he turned to theft, was caught in the act of stealing a pig and found himself under arrest for the second time. By an ironical twist of fate, he appeared in court before his old enemy Matthew Soames, and there was a dramatic confrontation. Joseph Smith could not resist taunting his old adversary, and Matthew Soames, whose temper was inclined to be choleric at the best of times, flew into an ungovernable rage, found him guilty (although the evidence was both scanty and suspect) and sent him back to gaol for a further three years. This sentence, to a man used to being free, was well-nigh insupportable, and Joseph Smith managed to escape on his way to gaol and make his way back to Shurdington, where he was caught parading up and down outside the house of Matthew Soames, playing on a pipe which was not his own and which he had probably filched. He was for the third time arrested, and charged with escaping his earlier arrest but, before he could be brought to trial, evidence of his rash statement to his cell-mate in Salisbury Gaol came to light and he was subsequently charged with witchcraft. Once again he came before Matthew Soames and this time the latter made no mistake, sentencing him with great relish to transportation for life. Thus, in due time, Joseph Smith was removed from Gloucestershire and from England, and shipped to the new state of Virginia on the eastern seaboard of the vast new continent across the wide Atlantic. And no more was heard of him.

Fussberger noted that the Reverend Hutchinson made only two comments in regard to this tale. One was that no irrefutable evidence of supernatural influences was ever found: a committee sent by King Charles himself conducted a thorough enquiry and discovered nothing. One authority suggested that the disturbances were engineered by one of the Soames family, or by one or more of the servants, although no adequate reasons for such behaviour were produced.

This was the end of the investigation as far as Fussberger was concerned. Soon afterwards his fiancée's father died, and with the inheritance he and his wife travelled to the United States and settled down in California; as far as is known, they did not return to these shores.

However, after studying the above fairly thoroughly, I feel that several additional points can now be made in view of more recent events. One is that the house of Matthew Soames in the seventeenth century *has* to be the one that was taken over by Mr Samuel P. Smith and occupied in 1906 – known as 'The Manse'. A second is to remark the coincidence (if coincidence it be) of the name of the flautist and of the American owner of the house centuries later: and to note that the former was transported to America and the latter came from there. Despite the fact that the name is extremely common in the Western world, was there, in fact, a family connection?

Lastly, the reason must be revealed why all the above mentioned has now been recounted. Earlier this year the Manse, once more a derelict ruin, was pulled down and, buried beneath the earthen floor in a stable built over a former outhouse, was discovered the remnants of a very old musical instrument, much corroded and blackened with age but nevertheless still recognisable, and pronounced by musical experts as being typical of the fifes in use circa 1650. It now reposes in a Cheltenham museum and I gather that to date there have been no strange noises from it, nor any other manifestations of the supernatural.

Perhaps the spirit of Joseph Smith, flautist, has finally come to rest.

IX

Guiting Forest

My last story is of particular interest, for at least four good reasons. One: it happened during the months of my researches for the rest of this collection; two: because it happened not too far from Cheltenham; three: because it deals with an aspect of the supernatural not covered up till now; and four: because it forms a fitting climax to what has gone before.

Enough preamble: on with the story.

Guiting Forest lies to the north of Cheltenham. It is possibly the largest tract of woodland in all Gloucestershire, barring the Forest of Dean. It covers a great many square miles, is dense in places, and contains a multitude of both coniferous and deciduous trees. There are pathways and tracks and bridle-paths running through it in all directions, many clearings here and there, the odd fir-clad rise and the occasional fern-clogged hollow. It abounds in wild-life and in the spring and summer can unfortunately be over-run by the human equivalent. The charming town/village of Winchcombe lies to the north-west, whilst Bourton-on-the-Water and Stow-on-the-Wold (mellifluous names indeed!) lie not far away.

There are few, if any, buildings actually located within the boundaries of the forest, but rural dwelling-places occur at intervals around the periphery. The home of Malcolm Coggeshall, his wife Brenda and his daughter Janice is one such, their actual address being 5 Abbot's Copse, Little Guiting.

159

Malcolm is the quality control manager for a firm of food processors in Cheltenham and, since his wife also goes out to work, they are able to afford a very nice house, fully detached, with four bedrooms, three living-rooms, two bathrooms, double garage and extensive gardens. Abbot's Copse is itself a very small settlement of newish houses, all about the same size but all very different in design, with fields to the south and woods to the west, and the forest to the north and east, stretching out like a dark green blanket into the hazy distance.

One bright Saturday morning in June, Malcolm Coggeshall came to me with an extraordinary story.

"I understand that you have a professional interest in local events of a somewhat bizarre nature?"

That was his conversational gambit.

"You understand correctly."

He pondered.

"Some . . . unusual things have been happening to me and my family very recently," he said after a lengthy pause.

"How recently?"

"Over the past week, in fact."

"Sounds promising. What kind of things?"

"Inexplicable things, at dead of night, in and around my home."

"Which is where?"

He gave me a note of his address, and added certain details concerning himself and his family.

"So you live on the edge of Guiting Forest?"

"My garden backs onto its southern edge."

"Before you plunge into your narrative, a drink?"

He nodded his thanks. As I prepared the refreshments, I studied him. He was slightly below average height, about forty years of age, fresh complexion, fair hair and blue-grey eyes. He looked an uncomplicated sort of man: not at all the sort of individual to whom 'bizarre' or 'unusual' happenings occurred. As I handed him his glass, I asked, "When exactly did it start?"

"As I said, a week ago – the night of June 13th actually."

"You're able to be that specific?"

"Oh yes. You see, that was the day my daughter and I dug up the skull."

The flicker of interest within me abruptly burst into flames.

"Did I hear you aright? You dug up a skull?"

"Yes."

"Human?"

"It looked like it. And I know *now* that it is."

"Male or female?"

"It's thought to be that of a male."

"And where did you dig it up?"

"In the forest, about a mile north of the house."

"This is very interesting."

"I guessed you might find it so."

"Have you been to the police about it?"

"Er . . . no." And, before I could make any comment, he hurried on: "When you hear my story, you'll know why."

"You'd better have a damned good reason." I paused, then added, "I take it this skull has something to do with these bizarre events you mentioned."

"They started that same night."

"Tell me about them."

He frowned in thought, his half-empty glass in his hand. Finally he looked me straight in the eye and said, "We think we're being haunted."

"By what or whom?"

"By the ghost of some large animal." He grimaced. "Either that or a man . . . person . . . on all fours."

"This gets distinctly more interesting every moment. How large?"

"Difficult to say. I'm the only one who has seen it more or less clearly: my wife glimpsed it through the window; my daughter hasn't seen it yet. Um . . . larger than a dog, smaller than a horse. Does that help?"

"Not a lot. You've no idea what kind of animal then?"

Once again he sat in silent thought, pondering earnestly. I got the impression that here was a man whose profession obliged him to choose his words carefully and he carried that same caution through into his private affairs.

"Could be . . . a large wolf."

"But you said you thought the skull was human?"

"So I've been led to believe."

Oh dear, I thought to myself, shades of Algernon Blackwood. Had Coggeshall been reading *Running Wolf* and had nightmares as a consequence? No, I decided, he didn't look the type. I said, "Sounds like you should tell me everything you can, right from June 13th."

He nodded. I replenished both our glasses and he began.

"June 13th was a Saturday. My daughter and I went into the forest to . . . er . . . well, to put it frankly, to remove one of the trees and transplant it into our garden. I will gloss over the criminal nature of the enterprise and will only say that in the opinion of the Coggeshall family the end justified the means."

He gave me a quizzical look that revealed an unexpected sense of humour.

"We soon found what we were looking for – a beautiful little silver birch, about ten feet high, with plenty of foliage. I had taken along a couple of short-handled spades concealed in a cricket bag – I play a bit, for my company team – and we began to dig, keeping an eye open for anyone out in the forest who might take exception to what we were doing." He had the grace to look slightly abashed. "We may not have been indulging in serious larceny, but we still felt a bit guilty. However, this did not stop us digging. Fortunately the soil was workable – no clay hereabouts – and we soon dug down two, three, four feet. I was surprised at the extent of the roots: there were plenty of them and they just seemed to go down and down and down.

"Well, to cut a long story short, at around five feet my spade struck something hard. I thought it might be a large stone, but Janice decided it was buried treasure and got a bit excited. I carried on digging and finally uncovered the object in question."

"The skull," I suggested, somewhat obviously.

"The skull," he nodded. "I was taken aback for a bit and Janice looked a trifle green, then rallied and told me to keep on digging in case there was a cache of ancient coins or jewellery or gold or whatever. I said that the only thing I was likely to find was more bones. Anyway, I disinterred the skull and carried on digging, but nothing more came to light, although I did manage to extract the tree, which we carried, together with the skull, back to the house."

He took a drink.

"I suppose I should have taken it to the police at once," he said. "For all I knew we might have discovered the remains of a murder victim. But . . . I didn't. The nearest police station is miles away, and my wife had the car (visiting her sister in Cirencester). I tried phoning them – the police, I mean – but kept on getting the engaged signal. And I was still trying to work out what I was going to say about our activities at the time: I guessed they would be frowned upon. So . . . I left it. I put the skull away in a cardboard box and tucked the box into a cupboard in my study. Brenda – my wife – got back from her sister's pretty late and we didn't get to bed until after midnight. Janice had gone up earlier."

He paused, as if to sort out his recollections of that night.

"I was woken up by my wife. She was shaking me by the shoulder. Wake up, she was saying, there's a dog or something out in the back garden making a horrible noise. He might be after the rabbits." Coggeshall gave me a wry grin. "The rabbits are Janice's latest fad and will probably last just about as long as all the others. At least it's better than punk rock. Anyway, I sat up and listened. A moment later I heard it as well – a very strange noise, a kind of low moaning howl: not the sort of noise a human throat could either utter or duplicate. I remember thinking: if animals have a hell, that sound came straight from it."

"What did you do about it?" I queried, to help the narrative along.

"I looked at the clock. It was two-fifteen. I got up and went to the window. It was pitch dark outside and I couldn't see a thing. A moment later that same eerie howl was uttered again, this time from a different direction. Whatever was making the noise was evidently moving around, either just beyond our perimeter fence or inside it, but not anywhere near the house. I went downstairs, found my hand-lantern, went into the lounge and shone the torch out through the patio door. It's a powerful beam and it lit up most of the garden, but I didn't spot anything moving, although there are plenty of trees and bushes to hide intruders. Janice made an appearance: she'd been woken up by the noise too. Whilst we were talking we both heard it again, the same long-drawn-out mournful lament, but in the distance! It's going away," I said. I opened the patio doors and Janice and I stepped out. It was a warm and overcast night, very quiet and peaceful, no moonlight to help us. We walked cautiously down the garden, flashing the torch-beam in all directions, over both side fences into the next-door gardens, and into the common land between our bottom fence and the forest.

"We saw nothing. We heard that dreadful howl once more, this time in the far distance – probably from the depths of the forest. After that, nothing. The next morning we asked around and found that most of our neighbours had heard it. Seems I was the only one brave – or stupid – enough to get out of bed and investigate." He chuckled for a moment, then sobered up. "One neighbour made what I thought was an interesting comment. He'd spent some of his earlier years in Canada and swore it was no dog he'd heard. More like a wolf, he said."

"You didn't connect this episode with the skull?"

"Not really. There seemed no reason to. Brenda made some remark about the coincidence of two unusual happenings on the same day, but we didn't think there was any connection – how could there be?"

Coggeshall drank the rest of his drink. I raised the bottle suggestively and in response to his nod refilled the proffered glass.

"On the following day – Sunday – I determined to take the skull the next day, as I assumed the police stations would all be closed on the Sabbath. Well, anyway, that was my main reason for not going as soon as I got up – that, and the fact I had a lot to do in the garden. But when Monday came I was tied up at the office with several meetings, and by Tuesday I was beginning to feel that it would be better to do nothing. There was the small matter of stealing Government property – which I assumed the tree was – and, if the finding of the skull *was* important, our names and address would be in all the papers and there'd be all kinds of notoriety and repercussions. Besides, one of my favourite mottoes is 'when in doubt, do nowt'. So I regret to say that is what I did."

"But obviously something more happened."

"Yes. On the Tuesday night. We'd had friends round – a business colleague and his wife and daughter – and I told them about the skull and showed it to them. Bill – my pal – was very interested. He has some slight knowledge of anatomy and *he* swore it was a man's skull. He even suggested it might be pretty old. You never know, he said, Guiting Man might become as famous as Neanderthal Man or Piltdown Man. I quickly reminded him that the latter had been a hoax, and this could be something similar. To me it didn't look all that old. He was strongly of the opinion that it might be the remains of a murder victim and recommended that I take it to the police asap." Coggeshall looked rueful. "He made me feel guilty and I determined to take it in the very next day.

"That same night we had the second incident."

He paused as though for dramatic effect and took a drink.

"Once again it was Brenda who heard it first. She woke me up and whispered in my ear that we'd got burglars. I was wide awake at once and looked at the clock: 1.30am. I asked her what she'd heard. She wasn't too clear about it: someone or something poking about at the back of the house; rustlings in the bushes; a sort of fumbling noise, at a door or window, or both; a weird noise, something like a large animal snuffling or grunting. I suggested the culprit might be Bill Sykes with a bad cold, but this didn't go down too well and she said somewhat tartly that I should see about getting up and protecting our property. I briefly mentioned the several burglary prevention devices scattered about the lower regions of the house, but she wasn't impressed. I went to the window and peered out. It was not as cloudy as Saturday night and a thin crescent moon gave a diffused silvery light. The garden was milky-dark and utterly deserted, silent under the stars. I went downstairs, treading quietly, disinterred a cricket bat from my bag in the cupboard under the stairs and headed into the lounge." He looked at me a trifle apologetically. "I'm no hero. I didn't so much want to capture the fellow as scare him off."

"I'd probably have felt the same way," I assured him.

He nodded. "I stood in the dark lounge and listened. Almost at once I heard what Brenda's keen ears had caught earlier: a low growling grunting noise, much as she'd described it. A big dog ferreting about, I thought with some relief. Then I heard a fumbling at the patio doors. I moved near to them and listened even more intently. Suddenly I saw the metal handle of the doors move downwards. Someone was trying to open them from outside."

Coggeshall looked at me quizzically.

"You can perhaps imagine what went through my mind at that moment! That was no dog turning the handle. Whatever was out there trying to get in had to be human. The next moment the handle was released and the doors shook, as though a heavy weight had been thrown against them. They weren't meant to resist such a weight. I knew that if it happened again the doors would give way."

He paused and took a drink.

"As I said, I'm no hero. I didn't know what to do for the best. Acting purely on impulse, I went to the light-switch, turned it on, then ran back to the patio doors, yanked the curtains aside and confronted whatever was out there with a raised bat and a fierce scowl." He chuckled. "I must have looked a bit like Geoffrey Boycott gone berserk."

"What happened?"

"The intruder beat a very hasty retreat."

I stared at him. "But you must have seen him?"

Coggeshall pondered on that one. "I saw something. Whether it was a 'him' or not, I can't be certain. An oblong of light was thrown by the lounge illumination onto the patio, and I thought I saw . . . a shape . . . escape from the light and run away down the garden. It ran so swiftly and so silently my eyes were unable to follow it. What it was I cannot in all honesty say. It seemed to me that it ran on all-fours, like an animal, and I had the impression it was large – much larger than a dog – and it was covered in hair . . . or fur."

"Yet you say it turned the handle of the patio doors."

"It's a metal handle, quite straight. I've heard of dogs – and cats – that have been trained to open doors with their paws."

I looked at him sceptically and he said, in a defensive manner, "I can assure you I was wide awake at the time, and *quite* rational."

"I don't doubt it for one moment."

"Besides, Brenda confirms everything I've told you."

"She does?"

"She was peering out of the bedroom window with the light off when I went into my mad cricketer act. She said that, as soon as the lounge light went on, she saw something leave the pool of light on the patio and run down the garden. She described it as a very large dog. Incidentally, we examined the fences next morning: there were no signs of something having broken in."

"Anything else?"

"One more thing. Two days later we had a burglary – or, rather, an attempted burglary. Another rude awakening, around 2am, when the damned burglar alarm went off. Living on the edge of the forest, and somewhat removed from civilisation – if that's what you can call it these days – we've had a fairly comprehensive alarm system installed. Every door and every window is wired to a central alarm fixed to the landing wall. When it goes off it makes one hell of a din and when it sounded at 2am, both Brenda and I were startled almost out of our wits. She immediately shrieked, 'Burglars!' and shoved me out of bed. I groped out to the alarm, switched it off and listened. In the ensuing silence I could hear my heart performing samba rhythms in my chest and I decided there and then to have a cardiac examination as soon as possible. Actually, on the whole I'm pretty fit but I must admit the old ticker was going nineteen to the dozen out there on the dark landing.

"Then I heard movements from downstairs. By this time Brenda had joined me, looking like a shapely ghost in her nightie, and a moment later Janice appeared, looking like a skinny wraith. We all listened and again the noise came – the sort of furtive fumbling sounds a burglar would make in the darkness. The two females looked at me for inspiration, but to tell you the truth I wasn't sure what to do. My only weapon of offence – my cricket bat – was downstairs, presumably near to where the burglar was moving about. Anyway, finally I plucked up courage and crept down the stairs, which fortunately don't creak. I paused on the half-landing and listened again. Then I heard what we'd heard on previous occasions – a low growling snarling sound. Immediately a picture flashed into my mind (and I *do* mean picture). It was a film we'd watched on TV about a tiger prowling through the jungle and the microphones had picked up the sounds made by the animal as it searched for prey. It was the same noise!

"The next second there was a loud splitting crack, just like wood snapping and splintering. It came from my study. All my property-protecting instincts came to the fore. I raced down the rest of the stairs, put on the hall light, groped in the under-stairs cupboard for my bat, grasped it in both hands and rushed into the study. There were startled movements from inside. I hurled the door open and felt for the light-switch. The damned door hit something soft, bounced back and knocked my hand away from the switch. All I had for illumination was the hall-light. As I stared in, boggle-eyed, my heart now performing like the percussion section of a Caribbean steel drum band, something appeared from behind the door, crossed the room in a flash, and leapt out of the open window. As this happened, something fell to the floor with a thud. For a second or two I was rooted to the spot, then I rushed to the window and looked out. The study overlooks the side of the house: there are flower beds and a path leading from the front gate, which was padlocked, to the rear garden. I thought I saw a dark shape flit swiftly down the lawn, heading for the bottom of the garden. And that's all I saw."

Coggeshall paused after his vocal efforts and took a drink.

"You say something appeared from behind the door and leapt

168

out of the window. Weren't you able to see what it was?"

He drew a deep breath and expelled it noisily.

"I wish I could say yes. It went very fast. I thought I saw . . . "
He shrugged. "I don't know. Human . . . or animal . . . or neither?
I can state definitely that it was upright, like a man. I say 'man'
because – I don't know why exactly – I felt it was powerfully
masculine. It was either naked and covered in hair or fur, or it was
wearing something like an animal-skin. It moved in total silence
and with amazing speed and it leapt out of the window with the
ease and pace of a jaguar."

"Is this the lot?"

"No. The next morning I examined the flower-beds below the
window. The soil was soft and moist and I found several prints.
Paw-prints, large ones."

I thought about his account for a minute or two, then asked,
"What was that you said about something that fell to the floor
with a thud?"

"Ah yes. I turned back into the room as Brenda and Janice
came down the stairs, calling out and asking if I was all right. I
told them I was and they came into the study and switched the
light on. It was then I remembered the thing that I had heard drop.
It lay on the carpet, gazing up at me with sightless eyes."

"The skull," I breathed.

He nodded. "The cupboard door had been forced open and the
cardboard box that had contained the skull was lying on the
floor."

"Presumably that's what your visitor was after."

"That *is* the inference one *could* draw," he replied, a trifle
formally.

"Anything else?"

"No. Except – I was talking with some friends and they
mentioned your name and what you do. I decided to come and see
you before taking any other action. It seemed to me you might be
able to advise me as to what to do next."

He looked at me expectantly. I drummed my fingers on the
table as I deliberated. Suddenly a point struck me.

"You said the . . . thing, whatever it was . . . leapt out of the

h

open window."

He nodded. "I wondered if you'd pick that up. When I examined it afterwards, I found it had been yanked open bodily, splintering the woodwork."

I stared at him. "No animal could do that!" I exclaimed.

"No ordinary animal, certainly," he responded calmly.

Once more I deliberated. Then I said, "Strictly speaking, you should take the skull to the police at once. But I'm not going to suggest that for at least two reasons. One: I have a vague feeling this is not exactly police business. And two: once they take charge of it you may never see it again, and it seems to me to be more than probable that it is the focus, if not the nucleus, of the unknown forces involved here. If you will permit me, I will telephone an acquaintance of mine who might offer some constructive help. His name is Reedman and he's the lecturer in anthropology at the local technical college. He used be at Leeds University. He lives not too far from here."

Receiving Coggeshall's willing assent, I rang Frank Reedman and arranged an early meeting. Because I had mentioned, briefly, the reason for the meeting, he suggested a rendezvous at the technical college. We agreed, and within the hour were ensconced in Reedman's small but comfortable office at the college. On the way we had detoured to Coggeshall's house to collect the skull in its cardboard box. Now, once the preliminary greetings and introductions were over, Coggeshall placed the box on the desk, without comment. Reedman, tall and thin, forty-five years of age, weather-beaten complexion, black-rimmed spectacles, neatly-trimmed beard, opened the box and stared at what lay therein. Then, with an indefinable expression on his face, he inserted his well-manicured fingers into the box and lifted out the skull. He examined it with minute care, looking at it from every possible angle, turning it over and over in his hands, completely absorbed in his task. After a good five minutes he looked at Coggeshall.

"Tell me where you found this."

Coggeshall made a succinct and honest reply.

Reedman placed the skull back in its box, walked over to an Ordnance Survey map of the area affixed to the wall.

"Would you care to indicate the precise location on this map, as accurately as you can please."

Coggeshall joined him and stood studying the map. Finally he reached out with a steady hand and touched a spot.

"As far as I can judge, here."

Reedman nodded. He came back to his desk and looked again at the skull. Finally he surveyed us (Coggeshall was once more by my side), glancing from one to the other.

"I'll need to make a few tests, check a few facts," he said. "It may take me several hours. Would you like to go away and have a leisurely lunch somewhere and come back here at, say, 3pm?"

We adopted his suggestion, and his recommendation of a certain hostelry a few miles away (which we found to be justified), and returned to the college precisely at three. Here we were given a message that Reedman was not quite ready and would see us in his office at three-thirty. We were provided with coffee and biscuits and were later conducted to Reedman's office, where we found him seated at his desk, several large volumes in front of him, the skull resting on one of them, facing him. With his beard and spectacles, he reminded me of sketches I had seen somewhere of ancient necromancers at their esoteric studies.

"What's the good news?" I asked as we sat down in front of his desk.

He gave me a slight smile, then stood up, leaned across the desk and proffered Coggeshall his hand. The latter, taken by surprise, shook it.

"What's that for?" he asked.

"Congratulations," responded Reedman jovially. "We have reason to suspect that you have made a most important find."

"Not another Peking Man," said Coggeshall sceptically.

Reedman laughed.

"Oh no. Nothing as ancient as that. This skull appears to be about four hundred years old."

"Old enough," I remarked.

"True. However, it's not its age that is so important." He leaned forward impressively. "We have . . . er . . . grounds for suspecting that this skull may possibly be that of the notorious Jess Butler."

171

Whilst part of my brain was querying just who Jess Butler was, another – more sardonic – was remarking the caution with which Reedman had made his statement. Almost every word or phrase he had used had been carefully chosen to be non-committal.

"And just who the heck is Jess Butler?" enquired Coggeshall.

"Was," Reedman corrected automatically. "You've not heard of him?" He looked at me.

I shook my head. "Well," I said. "Let us in on the secret. Who *was* Jess Butler?"

"He was – or at least was alleged to be – the werewolf of Guiting."

Coggeshall and I stared at the speaker in blank amazement.

"The who?" ejaculated Coggeshall.

"The what of which?" I exclaimed.

"It's a local legend," replied Reedman. "You've really not heard of him?" He gave me a comical look. "I should have thought you'd have come across it during your researches."

I shook my head.

"It sounds to me like a notable omission," I answered. "And a gap in my education that needs to be filled. Is it supposed to be true?"

He shrugged.

"It's like all other legends. Difficult to believe and impossible to prove. You can take it or leave it."

That sounded like something I've said in the past. Since it seemed we were on the same wavelength, I requested him to tell us about it. He gestured to the books on his desk.

"I rather thought that would be the case, so I've been reading up on it. But, before I start, how about some coffee?"

Whilst his secretary was providing the necessary refreshments, Reedman filled – and ignited – the contents of a pipe with a curly stem and a bowl carved into the shape of a bearded face. I wondered if he'd chosen it because of the resemblance to his own features. I looked expressively at the veils of smoke that drifted across the room like thin cloud across a plain, but forbore to remonstrate with him, not that it would have done any good.

Eventually Reedman told us the story. I took it down as he

spoke, and afterwards checked what I could, amended a few errors, and now set it down in more or less coherent and sequential form.

In 1582 the inhabitants of the small village of Guiting Power, set on the edge of the large area of forested country known in those days as Guiting Wood, were alerted to a danger that they had not before encountered – that of the possible presence of a large and ferocious animal within the forest.

They were first made aware of the threat when not one but several men stated that they had seen – or thought they had seen – a large wolf-like animal slipping silently through the darkened woods at dead of night. Since on each occasion there had been little moonlight, their stories were vague and unsubstantiated – especially in the case of one man who was known to be permanently inebriated and therefore highly unreliable.

But a little later evidence of a more spectacular nature was laid in a most brutal manner before the villagers. Three men, foraging through the trees in search of food, came across the dead body of a small boy aged about five. They were sufficiently horrified to observe that his throat had been torn out, but what was far worse was that the small body had been rudely stripped of clothing and the young white flesh had the appearance of having been *gnawed*. Despite their revulsion, the three men acted like good and faithful citizens: two stayed by the gruesome remains whilst the third made his way back to the village to spread the news and raise the alarm.

The boy was Tom Walsh, a crippled youngster who was only able to limp about with the aid of sticks and who must have been an easy prey for the marauding animal. It was asked how the boy had managed to find his way so far into the forest, but his sorrowing parents, little consoled by the fact that they had seven other offspring, told of the boy's love for the woodland glades and winding paths, a love that had led him to an untimely death. His father, a woodsman, organised a party of villagers and they set out to search the forest and to find and, if possible, to kill, the offending predator. They did not know what kind of beast they were hunting for, but they were not slow to connect it with the stories that had been circulating regarding a large animal in the neighbourhood.

Their search was neither skilled nor thorough, so that it was not surprising that it proved fruitless. No large animals were sighted, nor were any traces of one found.

Within the next two or three months the fears and suspicions of those living near to the forest were greatly exacerbated by several instances of groups of children being attacked by what was said to be a huge wolf. The existence, and indeed species, of the animal involved were no longer a matter of speculation: in each case the attack had been clumsily launched, and the children had had the time, courage and resource to scare away the attacker and escape back to the village with the news. After a number of such occurrences had come to light, the lord of the manor – at that time the Earl of Tewkesbury – organised properly-armed search parties and these men scoured the wood for traces of the prowler. But, just as before, nothing was found – no paw-prints, no droppings, no hidden lair – and after weeks of fruitless endeavour the attempts were abandoned, the concensus of informed opinion being that the animal had been frightened away from the area and had escaped to another county, hopefully never to return.

Alas, the hopes of the villagers, buoyed up by a few months of freedom from fear, were abruptly dashed when the body of a young girl was found, her throat torn out, her corpse stripped, and parts of her young body *eaten*. The girl, Maude Clark, had been a dull-witted child who had apparently wandered off into the wood without knowing why or where, and therefore she had been alone at the time of the attack.

By the time this dreadful news had been bruited abroad, further instances occurred. In each case a child on its own was assailed, throat torn out, body stripped, flesh eaten. The Earl was told: more search-parties were sent out: results were nil.

Then someone had a bright idea. Why not a small child as bait: allow him or her to roam the woods, with an armed band on hand in case the animal turned up? Nowadays such a scheme would not be entertained, but there were no child-care organisations around in the sixteenth century. The plan was adopted forthwith, a suitable orphan child procured from a nearby village, and the diabolical operation was set in motion.

The first time it was implemented, it failed in its purpose. But on the second occasion the small group of men, creeping silently through the forest some dozen yards behind the small child, were abruptly alerted by the sound of swift and violent movement through the undergrowth, followed by a horrific outbreak of growls and screams. They rushed forward with grim faces, grasping their weapons, and burst into a small clearing to find the child on the ground in a faint, and a huge wolf standing over her, manifestly about to attack her. When it heard the onrush of the men, it turned like lightning and, seeing its escape route blocked, backed against a group of trees, its visage a mask of feral hatred, its long sharp teeth exposed by the drawing back of the mouth in a snarl of defiance.

The men were pale but resolute. They held their pikes and halberds pointing forwards, their cudgels and axes aloft, and slowly they advanced towards the desperate beast. Unfortunately, one of the men stumbled over a concealed tree-root and sprawled on his face. The wolf reacted in a moment and made an enormous leap over the prostrate man. It eluded the weapons thrust at it and ran swiftly into the depths of the forest.

Whilst several of the men stayed to attend to the child, the rest stared at one another. Their feelings were mixed: relief that no one had been killed or injured (the child was found to be unhurt); terror at the recollection of the fierce hostility the animal had displayed, and baffled rage that it had escaped them. There appeared to be no point in pursuing it: a wolf can run much faster than a man. After a short discussion, they turned for home.

It was not until the party was nearing the edge of the village, one man carrying the child in his arms, that one of them, by name Ephraim Wimble, said out loud, quite suddenly and apropos of no previous remarks, "I be mortal a-feared. 'Tis my belief t'were no wolf we clapped our eyes on this day."

"No wolf," scoffed his friends. "What manner of foolishness is this, thou miserable poltroon?"

"Did none o' ye mark its features?" persisted Ephraim. "Did none o' ye see what I fear I seen? Did none o' ye mark how it looked like . . . "

"Who?" they challenged.

Ephraim licked his lips, peered about him fearfully.

"Jess Butler," he blurted out at last.

There was an awed pause, at the end of which another man – Henry Usher – whispered, "By all that's holy, Ephraim may not be wrong. T'was very like him."

Then another said. "As like as two peas in a pod, verily."

But others scorned and scoffed at the idea, and there was much argument as they returned to the village, with no satisfactory conclusions reached.

However, seeds of suspicion had been sown and soon dark rumours about the man in question began to spread.

Jess Butler was something of an enigma. He had arrived in the village a year before, from somewhere up north – some said as far away as Cumbria, or even Scotland. He was young – in his early twenties – with a saturnine face, small beady eyes and wild hair. It was noted that he moved around in a lithe animal-like lope, and he had been seen to raise his head as though sniffing the air, almost in the manner of a stag scenting for the proximity of enemies. His bearing was furtive, his temper short, and he admitted to no skills: consequently, when he settled in the area, no one would give him work. In the end he took himself off to an old abandoned hut in the forest and lived there, scrabbling somehow for a precarious livelihood. Somewhat later he took up with Martha Trench, the illegitimate daughter of a local farmer, a woman considerably older than he was, with an unprepossessing face and a bulky awkward body. They set up house in the hut and were joined in a desperate battle for existence and indeed survival.

This then was the man on whom suspicion, ill-founded or otherwise, now rested. Things grew to such a pitch that a few of the more venturesome and militant men from the village, emboldened by an enthusiastic intake of the local brew, went to the hut to confront Jess and cause as much mischief as possible. But so violently hostile and savage was their reception that they were driven away and discomfited to such an extent that they were too afraid to try again,

After this episode there came a lull in the reports of a wolf in the vicinity and the people in the area began to hope that the cause of all the trouble, wolf or no wolf, had at long last left the neighbourhood.

But, alas, this was not to be. There was one more act to the drama, and it occurred a week after the confrontation just recorded. A huntsman belonging to the Earl's huge estate – one Robert Catling – was riding through the forest with his wife riding pillion behind him. Without any warning a huge wolf bounded out of a thicket, leapt up at the woman with appalling ferocity, seized her right leg in its powerful jaws and pulled her bodily off the horse. Immediately it began to claw and bite at her. Catling, reacting with lightning speed, drew his long-bladed hunting-knife as he slid off his horse and without a second thought attacked the great beast.

At first the animal would not release its victim, and in fact its long sharp teeth had almost torn her leg off by the time her husband was able to do anything. He attempted to slash the animal's muzzle but was knocked over by its thrashing body. Leaping to his feet, Catling jumped onto the creature's back and plunged his knife into its shoulder. The wolf released the woman and whirled round to attack Catling. There ensued a short battle during which the beast tore open his left arm with its claws, whilst he was able to inflict another gaping wound, this time in its left foreleg.

At this stage the wolf appeared to realise that it was not going to win. With a final snarl of baffled rage, it backed, turned tail, and melted into the forest, although it moved with less than its normal speed, and it left a trail of bright red blood behind it. Catling did not pursue it: instead, he knelt down by his wife, and was thunderstruck to find her dead, possibly due more to shock than to the wounds inflicted on her.

The huntsman rose slowly to his feet, overwhelmed by a deep

grief that soon turned to a terrible rage. He bound up his injured arm, recovered his knife (wiping the blade clean on nearby grass), mounted his horse and set off in the direction taken by the beast. It had left a trail that was as plain as daylight to a man such as Catling, well-versed and fully experienced in the arts of hunting and the pursuit of animals, wounded or otherwise.

The trail led directly to the hut in the woods occupied by Jess Butler and his 'wife' Martha, thus confirming the rumours and suspicions that had been circulating in the area over the past few weeks. Catling tethered his horse to a tree, drew his knife and rushed at the door. He burst it open with one savage kick of his booted foot, ran inside, and found Jess seated naked on a stool, whilst Martha stood by his side attending to a bad wound in his shoulder – his *right* shoulder. His left leg had been roughly bandaged and blood was already seeping through the rough muslin. Jess's hair was even more wild than usual, matted and filthy, his hands and body bloody, his long finger-nails clotted with shreds of flesh and clothing. For a moment Catling was rooted to the ground with mingled amazement and horror. Jess Butler could do nothing but sag against the rough wall of the hut, too weak to move, but Martha drew back her thick lips to reveal long sharp teeth. She snarled with feral hatred, seized an axe and came at the intruder, her onrush all the more terrifying because of its silent ferocity.

Catling recovered his wits and mobility just in time. He managed to fend off her attack, but he too was weak from loss of blood. He turned swiftly and leapt out through the open doorway, ran to his horse, mounted, and rode as fast as he could back to the village. The alarm was immediately raised and an armed party rapidly assembled and made their way to the hut with all possible speed – only to find it empty, the couple flown. But once again the trail was not difficult to follow and the pursuers caught up with the fugitives in a clearing. Realising they were trapped, Jess Butler and his woman backed against a tree and snarled their defiance at the villagers, who formed themselves into a half-circle and advanced. After a short brutal battle the two wretches were captured and taken back to the village bound with thick ropes.

178

Since the charge was one of witchcraft – possibly the most terrible accusation that could be levelled at anyone in those superstition-ridden days – the prisoners were subjected to barbarous tortures. And it was whilst he was undergoing agonies on the rack that Jess revealed his true story which, to everyone's amazement, involved episodes of lycanthropy when he was but a child.

According to this pitiful victim of the torturer's 'art', he was only thirteen years of age when a friend of his father, by name Matthew Clarke, took him into the woods near his home (somewhere in Scotland: the exact location was never revealed) and introduced him to two sinister men dressed all in black. The larger of the two told the frightened youngster that, if he allowed him and his companion to perform certain arcane ceremonies there in the forest, with him as victim, including 'sundry acts of debauchery' (unspecified), their Master would turn him into a wolf. Jess was quite keen to be thus transformed, but rather less so on the conditions appertaining thereto. However, his base desires won and he submitted more or less willingly to the 'ceremonies' hinted at by the large man in black. At the end of the 'session' the leader's companion applied an ill-smelling salve to the boy's body and also marked his flesh with his long fingernails: and at the same time gave him a wolf-skin. From then on, according to the prisoner, he had enjoyed many times roaming the forest as a wolf, seeking victims. On one occasion he had snatched a baby from its crude crib and savaged it unmercifully. In every case he chose young children as his prey and he went about his foul purpose with such cunning that his depredations were put down to real wolves.

Then, one day, he became too bold. Three girls were walking through the woods when they came upon the boy, now fifteen, naked, hands red with blood, gnawing lumps of raw meat with undisguised relish. When, horrified, they asked him what he was doing, foolishly he boasted that he was a werewolf and was finishing off the remains of his last kill. The girls were terror-stricken and they ran away. The boy gave chase, but fortunately (for them) the girls encountered a band of gypsies who were armed with knives and out hunting for food. When the boy saw them he too ran away, but the gypsies pursued him, cornered him in a quarry and captured him. Acting with surprisingly good citizenship, the gypsies took him to the nearest town and handed him over to the authorities.

He was put on trial, but the local magistrates were unusually lenient, and they treated Jess Butler as a demented person rather than a criminal. He was of course found guilty, but because of his age he was not put to death but was sentenced to life imprisonment in a monastery on a remote island off the southern tip of the Hebrides.

He spent eleven years in the monastery and then managed to escape. He was seen attempting to swim away from the island towards the mainland and, because the weather that day was so foul, no boat set forth after him. When no more was heard of him, it was assumed that he had drowned. But of course he had not drowned. He was picked up by a fishing-boat which had been forced out of its usual fishing-grounds by the storm. When he had recovered from his near-death ordeal, he told his rescuers that he had been swept overboard from a large vessel which had then sailed on without him. The owner of the fishing-boat, a man from Cumbria, who handled the craft with the help of his two sons, accepted his story and in fact took him on as a third hand so that he could work his passage. Several weeks later they made harbour at Maryport, on the Cumbrian coast, whence Jess Butler departed in a southerly direction. He travelled at night, taking care not to arouse suspicion, working in return for food and shelter, all the time heading as far away from the north as possible.

Eventually he found himself in Gloucestershire and finding the county much to his liking, and not wishing to go any further, he took up residence in the hut in Guiting Forest. It had recently been vacated by a vagrant and left in such an appalling state that no one wanted it.

After a while Jess felt the need of a mate. For years he had been forced to forego the pleasures of the flesh, and since his escape his appearance and obvious poverty had denied him the

chance to satisfy his sexual appetite. But then he met Martha Trench. She was well past the age of 40 and nothing to look at, but she was available and she was willing. It is of course possible that he was subconsciously looking for a mother-substitute, whilst she may unconsciously have been on the look-out for the son she never had. Be that as it may (and Freud was hundreds of years in the future), they were attracted to one another and soon she had moved into the hut with him. Their unprepossessing appearance, uncouth manners and unsavoury habits ensured that their abode was shunned by the local inhabitants.

It was this same aversion felt for them that made it difficult for them to live anything other than a most precarious existence. No one would give them work, whilst what food they had was provided by Jess during his nocturnal expeditions into the woods that surrounded them on all sides. Their living conditions and their health deteriorated and their lives were a battle for survival.

Things were desperate indeed when, one night, during one of his many forays into the forest, he met up with two men on horses. Both wore black, as did their mounts. One was tall, thin and elderly: the other younger and bulkier. Amazingly, both appeared to know him, calling him by his name and in the next breath accusing him of breaking his contract with their master's servants many years before. They said it was time for him to renew his vows, once again to take up the manners and customs of a wolf, and in consideration of his willingness to do so they would grant him succour in his hour of need. Jess was nothing loath: he had not only grown weary of his struggle for a livelihood but also had, especially in the last few months, felt stirrings of his former bestial desires to slink wolf-like through the dark forest and to feed on human flesh. He therefore agreed. At a subsequent meeting he took part in a bizarre ceremony which involved him in diabolical excesses with the two men, in the frequent renunciation of God and Jesus Christ, and in kneeling naked on the grass whilst he kissed the uncovered fundaments of his mentors. Later a salve with a repugnant smell was massaged into his body and when he left them he was given coins of gold.

This time no wolf-skin was required. Whenever he exposed himself naked in the bright light of a full moon, he metamorphosed into a wolf and was able to roam the wooded countryside seeking victims. Later he grew so adept at his debased craft that he could effect the transformation from man to wolf at almost any time.

At first he was slow and clumsy and was seen by several men from the village so that he was obliged to run away. But one night he was fortunate (from his point of view) to come across a small crippled youngster limping along a forest path. The poor lad was paralysed with fright at the sudden appearance of the wolf and could neither resist or escape. This of course was Tommy Walsh, Jess Butler's first victim in the second phase of his dread disease. The resultant search made him give up his prowling for a while. But then he started up again and, after a number of failures when attacking groups of children, he learned to pick on youngsters on their own. Maud Clark was his second success and soon he was making 'kills' almost nightly. He also learned to devise means of evading search parties by lying low in secret hiding-places until the coast was clear for him to renew his fiendish activities.

Then came the experiment with the child from the orphanage and Jess's encounter with the men from the village, followed by the confrontation with him at his hut, where he and Martha put on a show of such savage hostility that the men were driven away. It made Jess realise that he had gone too far and accordingly he fought to stifle his bestial urges and give up his nocturnal wanderings through the forest.

But after a month or so the perverted lust that had bedevilled him ever since he was a boy boiled up again. Helpless in its vicious grasp, he assumed the mantle of a wolf and went out one more time into the forest to seek his prey. Unfortunately the prey he picked upon was the wife of Robert Catling. This was, as we know, one encounter too many, resulting in the capture and trial of both Jess and his 'wife' Martha.

On these confessions, Jess Butler was found guilty of all the charges, and Martha was found guilty of complicity. She was lucky: she suffered strangulation and her body was burnt on a bonfire. Jess Butler's fate – one of the severest ever known in

England – was chronicled thus:

> Jess Butler was suspended from a gibbet erected for the purpose, and sharp instruments were heated in hot coals and used to tear his evil flesh from his bones. After that his arms and legs were broken with cudgels, and then he was taken down and his head struck clean from his evil body, and his remains were burnt until only ashes were left, which were then scattered far and wide. His head was taken by the villagers and affixed to a tall pole which was then set up on the village green as a due warning to other potential lycanthropes. But a few days later it was gone from the pole, and despite some lukewarm investigation it was never ascertained who had filched the grisly relic, nor was it ever discovered what had happened to it subsequently.

When Reedman had finished his story, both Coggeshall and I were silent for a good minute. Finally Coggeshall said, "Have you any bona fide evidence to support any part of what you've just told us?"

Reedman smiled faintly and shook his head. He said, "A legend is an article of faith: it has to be accepted without question and without proof."

"An extraordinarily detailed and explicit legend," I remarked.

"Personally, I doubt if I believe one word of it," said Coggeshall. "I know very little of lycanthropy, but I venture to suggest that it is mainly a product of diseased minds. However, I owe it to my family to take any steps – however far-fetched – that might help to remove the threat to our home and our peace of mind." He looked at Reedman. "Will you take the skull off my hands?"

"You wish to transfer the burden to me?"

"I feel you're more equipped to deal with . . . anything that might happen. But, as I said, I'm deeply sceptical: I don't think there will be any more trouble."

"But what's your explanation of what happened at your house?"

"I have no explanation, except that I don't believe it had

anything to do with so-called werewolves, or indeed with anything supernatural."

Reedman turned to me. "What's your opinion?"

"As Christopher Isherwood was wont to remark, I am a camera. I prefer to record without comment."

"If you won't take it," said Coggeshall to Reedman. "I'll hand it to the police and they can do what they like with it."

"Don't worry, we'll take it. We still have tests to make on it."

As it happened, Reedman's tests were destined to remain incomplete. Three nights later the college was broken into, a locked cupboard forced open and the skull removed. It was never seen again.

Neither were there any further incidents connected with wolves, natural or supernatural, in Guiting Forest – or indeed in the whole of Gloucestershire. Which is perhaps just as well.